I'VE got a piece of advice for you," said Lucas McCain. "Don't hang around North Fork."

It was Trav Benteen standing before him, an old friend who had taken the outlaw road long ago. Now Trav wanted to stay awhile in North Fork. And Lucas McCain knew, even as he spoke, that all the words in the world wouldn't keep this dark-haired Texan from doing what he wanted to do.

Trouble stayed with him. Robbery and shooting were everyday occurrences, and suspicion walked the streets—suspicion of anyone who had ever known Benteen. Young Mark McCain learned what it was like to sit up all night waiting for raiders to attack—knowing the only defense was the rifle that never left his father's side.

Mark wanted to pull his own weight as half of the McCain partnership. But it was not until the Texas outlaw made his most desperate play, and a little girl's life was in danger, that he got his chance. What happened then makes a thrilling climax to this dramatic story of The Rifleman—a man who is building a fine future for himself and his son and is willing to fight for it.

"The Rifleman"

"The Rifleman"*

Based on the television program
starring Chuck Connors as *Lucas McCain*

By COLE FANNIN

Illustrated by
HENRY LUHRS

*Trademark

WILDSIDE PRESS

CONTENTS

"The Rifleman"

1   Benteen Comes Back

Everything was as right as it could be, that warm May morning, until Mark McCain encountered the men who had built a fire against the big cottonwood by the river.

Mark felt good because school was out and the long summer stretched ahead, when he would work the ranch with his father, Lucas McCain—the man whom some in the town of North Fork and thereabouts had started calling the Rifleman, because of the beautiful and deadly long-gun which was always close to his hand.

Mark's sorrel pony, Latigo, snorted and took the high grass near the river at a run, his mane rippling, with the wind hard from the north in Mark's face. Latigo obviously felt good too.

Yes, everything was fine. It was a good year. There was promise the ranch would soon be returning a profit. That

morning after breakfast, his father, smiling, had said, "It
looks like we McCains are making good here, son!"

We McCains. That had made Mark's chest swell until
he was in danger of popping his buttons. It was Lucas
McCain's way of doing things. They were partners here.
Lucas never made a move without gravely consulting his
son.

They shared everything. Including the work, of course.
Lucas had said, after breakfast dishes were washed and
put away, "Got to line up the day's chores now. Mark, you
go check the intake gate at the river, see the water is flow-
ing good. I'll take a look at those two-year olds in the south
pasture that we'll soon be moving to market. When you're
finished, come join up with me."

They had parted outside the barn, Lucas moving away
at an easy lope on his black Razor, sitting tall, rifle resting
across saddle horn. Mark headed Latigo north, beside the
irrigation ditch, dug with so much sweat and backache but
bringing water to the pastures and to the truck garden near
the house which was Mark's chief responsibility.

The water level in the ditch seemed good, but Lucas
had said to check the gate, and Mark rode on to do it. Then,
cutting across the north pasture, he saw the smoke ahead

and knew a moment of heart-squeezing fright.

Fire was about the worst danger any ranch had to face. Let it get a foothold in the grass, curing so early this year, and it could sweep right across the place. Mark worked through the screen of timber along the riverbank, guiding Latigo with rein and knee, and saw it was a cook fire, built against the big cottonwood that stood just west of the water intake gate.

Several men were moving around. Mark counted four of them, all rough looking, wearing range gear. Their horses were off to one side, close-tethered, nuzzling at the grass.

The men had obviously just finished eating breakfast, judging by a coffeepot set close to the fire, by a skillet and tin plates and cups scattered about. As Mark reined Latigo down, one of them whipped around, a gun flashing into his hand. It leveled right at Mark, with the hammer clicking back.

For a second, Mark felt very scared again. You couldn't live in this country and not be pretty familiar with men packing guns and what some of those men might do with them, for very little reason or none at all.

But he sat his saddle without flinching, and the moment

passed. The man snorted, letting the hammer down again, shoving the gun into a holster at his hip. "Only a kid!" he said.

Mark felt a touch of anger. It was partly because of the tone in the man's voice, the curl of his lip, and partly—well, some people you just didn't care much for, on sight, and this was one of them, a man who was lean and tough-sinewed, with nothing but hardness about him—hard eyes, hard jaw, hard mouth.

In addition, there was the fact that Mark didn't at all like being called a kid. Maybe he wasn't very old, but he was trying to grow up as fast as he could and had thought he was making pretty good progress.

He wore saddle breeches and boots and a curled-brim hat, just like Lucas. He handled his share of the riding chores as well as any hired puncher could—Lucas had said so. Mark figured he wasn't much of a kid any longer and shouldn't be called one.

"My name's McCain," he said. "And this is McCain land you're on. Not that you aren't welcome to light and rest awhile. But you shouldn't have built your fire against the tree. It has already taken hold. If it eats in, the tree will die. Also, there's danger of its spreading to the grass—"

The man was staring at him. He had sandy hair, and eyes so pale there didn't seem to be any color in them at all. Suddenly Mark McCain found himself remembering something Micah Torrance, the town marshal at North Fork, had once said: "Whenever I see a gun-toter with light-colored eyes, I'm extra careful. That kind, I've learned, is real dangerous. I learned it the hard way too."

The man said softly, "You telling me to put that fire out, kid?"

One of the others, looking on and listening, spoke up, "Ah, don't hooraw him, Cade. You know what Benteen said—no trouble—"

So the man with the light-colored eyes was named Cade. He said, without even looking at the man who had spoken, "You shut up!" And, to Mark, "Give me an answer!"

Mark found himself trembling inside. But he was determined not to show this. He said, "I'm asking you to do it, since you've finished your breakfast and don't need the fire any longer." Then he added, "Please."

Cade smiled. It was a cold sort of smile, with his lips barely twitching. "Please! Real polite, aren't you? And I hate polite squirts!"

The other men were standing, not saying anything. It

seemed pretty evident they weren't going to take a hand, one way or another, probably because they didn't want any part of tangling with Cade.

Mark knew he was in a tight. He gave a moment's thought to jabbing his heels into Latigo's flanks, turning the pony, getting away from here as fast as he could ride. But he didn't do this. Lucas had said when a man got himself into a tight he should work his way out of it, not do any running.

So, instead, Mark dismounted, letting his reins drop to the ground. Latigo had been trained to stand. He said, "I'll do it for you, Mr. Cade," and started for the fire.

He scuffed dirt with his boot and shoved it on the flames, taking care that none got in any of the utensils scattered about.

Before Mark could kick any more dirt on the fire, Cade's hand gripped his shoulder. Cade jerked him around, lifted him up on tiptoes, and shook him hard. Then he gave Mark a shove which sent him staggering aside. Mark landed on one knee, against the ground.

"I'll let you know if I want that fire out!" Cade said bitingly.

The others still didn't say anything. Cade bent and

picked up a burning branch from the blaze which was eating into the big cottonwood. Mark noticed he did this with his left hand, leaving his gun hand free.

He looked then to Mark, and his eyes seemed to go a little murky.

"Water running in a ditch, fences, a garden patch yonder —it's all got the looks of a hoeman's spread," Cade said. "And I hate every hoeman alive!"

He turned the branch, making it flame more briskly. "So you're afraid of fire loose in your grass, kid," the man said. "Well, I'm of a mind to get one started—just to watch you try to stomp it out—"

"No!" Mark cried and started to rise.

"Stay put!" Cade said. "I'll tell you when you can get up!"

One of the other three men stirred, then. "Now, listen! You're going to get all of us in trouble with Benteen—"

"I told you to shut up!" Cade snapped at him. "Maybe you're afraid of Trav Benteen. I'm not!"

"Aren't you, Cade?" somebody said, from behind Mark. "Try telling me that—to my face!"

It was a man who had come along so quietly Mark had not heard him at all. Neither, obviously, had Cade, who stared at the newcomer. "This is a private matter, Benteen, between me and a mouthy kid—"

"Nothing's private, in my bunch," the man called Benteen said. He glanced then at Mark. "Stand up, boy. Tell me what got you crossways with Cade."

Mark stood up. He told quickly why he had come along, the fire and the damage it could cause if it did any spreading. Benteen listened, studying him intently. He was a big, dark, heavy-set man with handsome features. His gear was much better than that of the others, though Mark noticed places where it had been patched and mended.

"I see," Benteen said, when Mark had finished, without saying anything about Cade's threat to fire the grass. Then the man continued to study Mark. "You've got a familiar look, as though we'd met somewhere . . . ."

Benteen shook himself, turning to Cade. "The boy is right. Kill the fire."

"Not me!" Cade snapped. "You want it out, do it yourself!"

"No. You'll do it," Benteen told him.

He put a hand on his gun, a pearl-handled Colt .45 in a hand-tooled leather holster, hung from a shell belt which had all its loops full. Mark noticed the gun was tied down, with a leather thong about Benteen's thigh. He remembered something Micah Torrance had once said about men who tied their guns down—that they needed close watching too.

"I told you, Cade, when you joined up with me and my bunch two days ago, that you'd take my orders," Benteen said. "Now you'll do it, or get out. Kill that fire!"

Cade still held the burning branch. His right hand brushed the handle of his own gun, tied down also. "You'd take the side of a hoeman's kid, bother about what might happen to a hoeman's spread?" he demanded.

"I'm not planning to cause useless trouble that might have the whole country coming at us!" Benteen said.

"Well, if you want that fire put out, you'll do it yourself," Cade told him. "And I'm still of a mind to spread it through that grass—"

Mark held his breath. It was plain some sort of showdown was imminent here, due to explode in another second, each of these men drawing their guns.

But it didn't happen, because Lucas McCain came along.

Razor, his black, moved at a quick rush through the trees, was reined to a halt and Lucas was out of saddle and standing beside Mark, all in one easy motion. He held the rifle with his right hand, finger on the ring, muzzle pointing to the ground.

He took in everything. To Benteen he said, in his quiet manner but with a tension in his voice that Mark instantly noticed, "Hello, Trav."

Benteen started. His eyes narrowed, his mouth rounded for a moment as his glance flickered from Lucas to Mark, then back again. "So that's it! He's your son, Lucas. Had a feeling I'd seen him somewhere before. It was Margaret I was seeing. He takes after her, a lot."

Lucas' mouth tightened a little, the way it always did when somebody mentioned Mark's mother. "I guess he does," Lucas replied.

"You're a long way from the Nations and the trail across Red River," Benteen went on.

"So are you, Trav," Lucas said.

"That's right," Benteen agreed, smiling. "We've both wandered a far stretch from where we first met."

"But following different trails," Lucas said, the tension still in his voice.

Benteen's smile persisted. "Well, Lucas, I always had a different ambition than the one driving you. It didn't include sitting down on a patch of grass and taking root, which it looks like you've done."

"I know," Lucas said. "You wanted big money to spend, and you wanted it in a hurry." He sized the other man up. "Doesn't look like you've had much luck—"

"Oh, I've done all right, at times," Benteen said, his smile now fading somewhat. "Had a rough winter up north at Deadwood, though, with pickings kind of thin—"

"A tough new marshal at Deadwood, I've heard, who makes pickings thin for everybody," Lucas interrupted.

"Maybe," Benteen said. "Me and my bunch, we're looking for more promising country."

Cade, who had been listening, his glance shuttling between the two, now broke in: "Enough of this gab!" he said.

He moved a couple of steps closer to Lucas, a move which put Lucas between himself and Benteen. His eyes were murky again as he looked Lucas up and down, insolently. "This is the kid's dad . . . the hoeman!" he said.

The others shifted position, muttering. Nobody in range country had any use for a hoeman, a farmer. Even Benteen stood silent, frowning.

Lucas McCain looked Cade up and down also. "You're mistaken," he said. "I'm not a hoeman."

"You say!" Cade jeered. "The look of your place yonder says different!" He glanced around at the other three. "How about it? Who's with me to start his grass burning, clean him out—make room for an honest cattleman to run his stock on this graze?"

The men shifted about again, with louder muttering. It wouldn't take much more, Mark realized, to put those three on Cade's side, have them backing him up in what he was proposing to do.

Lucas said, voice cold and quiet, bitingly, "That word 'honest' has a mighty queer sound, coming from the likes of you. And I've got some advice you'd better heed. Don't talk about burning McCain grass . . . don't try doing it!"

Cade snorted. "You're as mouthy as your kid! And nothing to back up your talk but that rifle—which you'd sure better hold right where it is! Because if you make any move at trying to use it, I'll fill you full of bullets before you can ever get it leveled at me!"

Lucas looked him up and down one more time. "You're the mouthy one here," he said, voice colder still. "And I've learned that the biggest waste of time and effort in this world is to try to convince your kind of anything. You have to be shown—"

Lucas' voice chopped off then, and he made his move, the rifle snapping up, his left hand flashing to steady it, his hand pulling the ringed lever.

Mark had seen his father do it before, but the move was always too fast for him to follow. Lucas was pouring out bullets so rapidly their explosions seemed one continuous roar—straight at Cade.

The man didn't have a chance to reach for his own gun, not a chance on earth. And Lucas was deadly accurate with the rifle. At any distance up to a hundred yards he could put his bullets into a target no bigger than a man's palm. Mark had seen him do it.

2   A Second Offer

Cade let out a wild scream of fear, with the rifle's powder flame lashing at him from a dozen feet away, the bullets screaming past his face. He hit the dirt on his stomach and groveled there, clawing at the ground as though trying to dig a hole and hide himself.

Lucas had not, of course, been aiming to hit him. He couldn't possibly have missed, if that had been his intent. He had meant only to put his bullets fairly close—and had done so.

The crashing reports echoed through the timber and died away, with an acrid haze of powder smoke eddying in the air, as Lucas stopped firing. But his hand was still on the ring as he grimly sized up the others.

"Four bullets spent—and I'm using a Henry magazine, which means seven bullets left," he said. "Now, does anybody else have notions about setting fire to McCain grass?"

Nobody moved or spoke. They all seemed frozen as they stared in awe at the rifle.

Cade, sitting up, was slapping frantically at his ducking jacket which was smoldering. He had fallen on the burning branch.

Benteen laughed. "Don't worry, Lucas. You convinced them plenty!" he said. Then he raised his voice. "Get the gear loaded and the horses ready. We're pulling out of here. But first, Cade, like I told you before, go kill that fire!"

Cade sent a bitterly corrosive look at him. Then he looked at Lucas McCain, a look which told Mark the man would never forget that moment when he had sprawled on the ground.

Cade lifted himself. Head down, he went to the fire and began kicking dirt over it.

Benteen went on, "Lucas, it doesn't matter to me, but the *zanja* yonder and what I saw of your place makes it sure look like you've turned hoeman."

Mark had heard Lucas use the word *zanja* also. In Spanish it meant irrigation ditch.

"Easier than toting water to the house, that ditch," Lucas

told him. "And cheaper than drilling a well."

"Fences around your place—wire," Benteen said.

"Some wire," Lucas admitted. "We run about fifty head of cattle, mostly yearlings. I figure that fencing a pasture and keeping them penned up builds beef faster and makes them easier to handle than having the stock scatter for miles the way they will, hunting their own grass."

"That truck garden yonder?" Benteen said.

"We raise potatoes, roasting ear corn, green stuff for the table," Lucas told him. "I've seen scurvy in cow camps where the only grub was beef and beans. I mean to keep my teeth, mean to see Mark does too."

Mark was moving about, picking up the four empty cartridge cases. Lucas would reload them, measuring powder almost to the grain, tamping in lead that he molded himself.

"Well, I guess you haven't turned hoeman, all right," Benteen laughed. "Except what grubbing you must have to do to keep the garden weeded."

Mark started to speak, to explain that it was his job, and not Lucas', to weed the garden. But Lucas, with a glance, kept him quiet.

Cade had finished putting out the fire. He went sullenly

to get his horse, his face a dull red.

And Benteen continued, now eyeing the rifle, "Never thought you'd switch to a long-gun, Lucas, not when I remember how fast you used to be with a Colt."

Lucas motioned with his hand for Mark to climb saddle, and Mark went to pick up Latigo's reins.

"I can see the reason, now," Benteen said. "You're faster with that rifle than all but the fastest draws are with a hand-gun. And it gives you more distance. I can't hold true with my .45 much past fifty yards. But I'd bet you could drill a dime at a hundred. It gives you a big advantage over almost any man coming against you."

"I use it as a tool, Trav," Lucas said. "Against wolves and coyotes, mostly. They drift south across the river, especially in winter."

One of the other men brought Benteen his horse. It was a big black animal, nervous and fidgety. Benteen held it with a firm grip on the reins.

"What kind of rifle is that?" he asked. "Thought it might be a Winchester, at first, but I see now it isn't."

"Winchester-type barrel," Lucas said. "I made most of the gun—barrel, stock, trigger and ejector action—myself."

"You always were right clever at working metal—and

leather and wood too," Benteen said. Then, "Lucas, I know places where you could earn a couple of hundred a month —and more—with that rifle. Interested?"

"You know what I think of hired guns," Lucas said. "I'll never hire out mine."

"Well, you're probably right . . . could pick yourself up ten times as much, other ways. Like riding with me—"

Cade made an angry sound at this. Benteen frowned at him. "Get going," he ordered. "All of you. I'll catch up."

They started to trail slowly away, west along the riverbank. And Benteen's attention returned to Lucas, who said, "Trav, we had it all out a long time ago. I told you then I'd never ride with you again. That still stands."

For a moment, Benteen's eyes were shining and hot with anger. He was facing Lucas, the two men standing close together; and Mark noticed how Lucas, who topped six feet five, stood several inches taller than Benteen. But Lucas was also lean, and Benteen weighed at least thirty pounds more than he did.

"Maybe that's the way it stands right now, Lucas," Benteen said. "But you might change your mind—and you might be doing it before very long."

Lucas said, voice suddenly tight, "What does that mean,

Trav—that you're not riding on?"

"I've heard about your town of North Fork. It just might be that me and my bunch will stay around here for a while, look it over," Benteen answered.

He turned then and swung into saddle on his big black. From the way the lines showed in Lucas' face, Mark knew he was worried. "Trav," he said, "I've got a piece of advice for you: Don't do any hanging around North Fork."

Benteen laughed, gathering his reins. "Never was much good at taking advice!" Then he hesitated. "Lucas—you had any word lately from—well, down home?"

"Texas?" Lucas replied. "No. Not for nearly six months. Why? Have you been expecting some word from there?"

"No," Benteen said. "Just wondered if there was any news."

He rode away. Lucas stood for a minute, looking after him, then went to be sure the fire was completely out. After that he made his easy swing to Razor's saddle and glanced at his son. "Did you check that intake gate?"

Mark heeled Latigo and rode hurriedly on along the bank. He found the gate open and the flow good. The river sparkled in the day's hot sunlight, still with a high level, though there would be a lot of sandbars showing, come

August, with little water in the ditch at all. But by then the hay would be in for winter feed and the root cellar full of supplies for the cold months.

Mark doubled back through the north pasture and caught up with Lucas, who was riding with his reins slack, deep thought showing in his face.

They moved along together for a bit without speaking, while Mark thought of all that had happened. Presently he cleared his throat. "I—I guess I made a mistake, didn't I?" he said.

Lucas glanced at him, with a slow nod. "I'm glad you see it for yourself, son," he replied.

They both understood—without having to go into detail, the way it frequently was between them—that Mark shouldn't have ridden up to the fire the way he had. Not with men there of the calibre riding with the man called Trav Benteen.

Mark said, "I was afraid of the fire spreading to our grass."

"I know," Lucas said. "But I'd rather have the grass burn than have you in trouble with men like that. Don't take such a chance again, Mark—particularly not with them, if they should happen to show up again."

This meant Lucas was afraid they hadn't seen the last of those riders.

They continued to ride along together, at a slow pace. Their place appeared before them: the small house and barn and corral, set in a shallow sort of swale for protection against the wicked wind from the north in winter, with a background of green timbered hills.

A lot of work had gone into the place. Both of them were very proud of it. Did the coming of Benteen and Cade and those others mean it was in danger?

Mark cleared his throat again. "That Mr. Benteen—you knew him . . . well, before?"

"Yes," Lucas answered. "We met in the range country below San Antonio, made two trips together up the Chisholm Trail through the Nations with big cattle herds. Benteens and Porters—your mother's folks, son—were close neighbors. For a while, I figured Travis Benteen was my best and closest friend. . . ."

Lucas had a sort of far-off look which always came to him when he spoke of the Nations and Texas. Mark had no memory of either of them. Lucas had promised they would visit those fabulous places some day. Mark looked forward to that, a lot.

He felt considerably puzzled, because friendship meant a great deal to Lucas who had said a man should pick his friends with great care and then stick with them through thick and thin, good times and bad.

But something had happened to end the friendship between Lucas McCain and Travis Benteen.

Mark figured that if Lucas wanted to tell him about it, he would. And Lucas did.

"Trav itched for money, a lot of it, in a hurry," Mark's father explained. "Drawing puncher pay, saving up, buying grass and building a ranch—all that was too slow for him. There was only one way to get what he wanted. That was to take it away from somebody else, with a gun in his hand—"

Lucas tightened reins, then, and gigged Razor to a faster pace. Mark did the same with Latigo.

"It's awfully hard, trying to figure how far you should go with a friend who turns bad," Lucas continued. "I stood by Trav Benteen through a couple of scrapes that he brought on himself. Then it became plain that if I tried to stand by him any more than that, I was going to have to ride the same trail he was following, whether I wanted to or not. So I had to tell Trav that we were finished."

Such a decision must have hurt, from the expression on Lucas' face. They rode on for several minutes in silence, through the high grass. Then Mark said, "You think that —well, maybe he might cause you some trouble now— here?"

He was thinking of what Benteen had said about Lucas McCain joining up with him again, because of something which might happen soon.

"Hard to tell," Lucas answered slowly. "Trav was always a great one for making talk. It could be that's all he was doing, that we'll never see him again."

Mark hoped his father was right. He had no desire to encounter Trav Benteen again—or the man called Cade. Then Lucas grinned, glancing down at his son.

"Too nice a day to be worrying about things that might never happen," he said. "Come on, let's go take a look at those two-year-olds!"

They were plenty busy through the balance of the day. Lucas decided that about a dozen of the fat young steers were ready for market. "The buying price for such prime stuff is steady at around twenty-five, which means we can sell, restock with yearlings, and still have some money to put in the cashbox," he told Mark.

It meant cutting out the animals Lucas selected, moving them from the fenced pasture and shaping them up for the drive to North Fork—not an easy job, for the cattle weren't eager to leave their good graze.

Lucas assigned himself to do the holding and let Mark do the cutting, a job which he thoroughly enjoyed. Latigo enjoyed it too, with the quick turns and twists needed to handle the young white-faces when they tried to dodge away, double back.

"You're working into a real good cutting hand, son," Lucas told him, praise which made Mark beam with pride. Then his father added, as he usually did, lest Mark form too high an opinion of himself, "But you must learn to handle them a mite more gently. No need to tire stock out when you're planning to put them on the trail."

What with one thing and another, it was well into the afternoon before they were on the road to North Fork, and past sunset before they reached the loading pens there near the river. Lucas took the drag, at the rear, and let Mark handle the point, leading the small herd, out in front.

Once under way, the cattle moved along in fairly docile fashion at a shuffling trot, kicking up dust. It wasn't far to

North Fork, about five miles west, but Mark covered at least three times that distance, on Latigo, what with having to veer away and haze back those adventurous animals which did try to break free.

Mark enjoyed all this. He could imagine himself on the Chisholm Trail, like Lucas in years past, with a herd of a thousand head to look after instead of only a scant dozen.

When the cattle were penned, Lucas said, "I'll go dicker the sale now. Suppose you visit around, and we'll meet in about an hour at the Madera House for supper. I figure we've earned ourselves a meal there."

Supper in town was a real event. Mark anticipated it happily as he rode on into the bustling little town where lighted lamps were beginning to twinkle.

On the main street he dismounted in front of the small frame building used by Marshal Micah Torrance as his office and jail. Mark went inside.

Micah, busy at his desk with some paper work, looked up with a welcoming smile. He was a lean, weathered, soft-spoken man. "Howdy, Mark. Is Lucas with you, or is this just a solo visit?"

Mark told him Lucas would be along and that they would be having supper at the Madera House. Micah said, "Good.

Maybe I'll be joining you." His attention returned, frowningly, to a paper he had been studying. "Got something I want to talk to him about—"

That was when the guns started roaring, off toward the north, the direction from which Mark had just come— first the deep-toned explosions of .45's and then, cutting in, the sharp, fast firing of Lucas McCain's rifle.

Micah moved fast, but not as fast as Mark. He was first through the door, leaping to saddle on Latigo, whipping the pony around, then driving hard back to where his father had run into trouble.

3   Mark Finds Out

It was almost dark. An embankment, raised to fight some past flood, blocked Mark's way. He sent Latigo flying up it.

Down beyond, at the near end of the loading pens, was a cluster of small shacks used as offices by the cattle buyers. The door of one was open, with lamplight from within spilling out. Mark saw Lucas standing just outside the door, light against him and his rifle half-raised, looking off toward the west.

Lucas became aware of his son. He called, "Stay back, Mark!"

Micah came along, then, to halt and dismount. He went on afoot, calling, "You all right, Lucas?"

"Yes," Lucas answered. "Sam Bullard isn't, though. He's just inside—stopped a bullet."

Sam Bullard was the buyer with whom Lucas generally did business. Micah looked around at Mark. "Get some more speed out of your pony, son; go tell Doc Harvey he's needed here. Hurry!"

Some onlookers, drawn by the shooting, were gathering along the embankment. Mark turned Latigo and crossed it again. He took the first side street to the south, reined down in front of a white cottage, and ran along a gravel path to hammer at the door.

Dr. Dan Harvey, a pleasant young man new to North Fork, opened it, with his wife peering over his shoulder. He was the only physician in town, now that Dr. Burrage was away on a visit east. In his shirt sleeves, Dr. Harvey shook his head ruefully as Mark told what had happened.

"Haven't been able to finish any supper this week! Mark, will you go bring my bay around front—he's already saddled—while I get my bag?"

They rode back together. More people had gathered along the embankment, but Micah's night deputy had come on and was keeping them out of the way.

Dr. Harvey went into Sam Bullard's office. Mark held his bay for him. Lucas and Micah came out, to stand nearby. They had been working over Bullard. Now Lucas was telling everything that had happened.

"I stayed on for a few minutes at the pens, after Mark left, making sure the cattle were comfortable and had plenty of water," he said. "Then I came on toward Sam's place, noticed his lamp was burning. It looks," Lucas glanced around, "like the other buyers quit for the day and went home . . . ."

Their windows were dark, all right.

"Saw somebody open his door and go in," Lucas continued. "Then Sam yelled and the first shot sounded. I started to run forward. Two men came out, moving fast. Both had bandannas over their faces. I called for them to stop. They burned some bullets at me, and I burned a few back. Pretty dark, though. They didn't touch me, and I had no feel of scoring any hits on them."

"Recognize those two—or either of them?" Micah asked.

"Not for sure. They ran—had horses in that clump of willows near the river—hit saddle and headed for yonder, riding west. I went into Sam's place, found him on the floor, all his pockets turned out—"

"He probably lost plenty," Micah said. "Confound it, I've warned all the buyers about those big bank rolls they carry with them!"

"They usually have to do spot cash business, which means they must pack big rolls," Lucas said. "And it makes them prime targets, of course, for stick-up men."

"That's right," Micah agreed. "Hold up a cattle buyer at this season, you're liable to make a bigger haul than if you hit a bank!"

Dr. Harvey appeared in the doorway, then. "Bullard will be all right," he reported. "Will have to spend some time in bed, though, and he's yelling his head off about that, what with the first trail herds from Texas about due. He's afraid that he'll lose a big chunk of that business."

This reminder that the trail herds would soon be passing through North Fork made Mark tingle inwardly. It was the most exciting time of the year when the Texas cattle began to arrive, cowpunchers thronging the streets and telling their tales of wild adventure on the long trail from the south.

"He's probably right," Micah commented. "Poor Sam! He not only got robbed, but will be flat on his back when those Texas ranchers are selling their herds."

Bullard was brought out presently, carried by four men on an improvised stretcher. They moved off in the now thick darkness toward his home.

The buyer spoke weakly, as he was being borne away, "Thanks, Lucas. And don't worry about your two-year-olds. I'll pay for them, soon as I can sign a bank draft."

Dr. Harvey had a smiling word of thanks for Mark. "My wife tells me you haven't been around lately to test her apple pie. Come see us as soon as you can."

"I will," Mark promised, though it wasn't apple pie that interested him in Mrs. Harvey's kitchen, but cake. The doctor's wife, sworn to secrecy, had been teaching him how to bake one, for a very special reason.

This left only Micah and Lucas, along with Mark. The two men started pacing back and forth, talking low-voiced. But their words were audible to Mark.

Micah said, "Lucas, I've got to ask you a question. Could one of those two men who shot Sam Bullard and robbed him have been Trav Benteen?"

"That's a sort of unusual question, Micah," Lucas said. "Mind telling me why you asked it?"

"I've had some reports about him, that he got in trouble up at Deadwood, is wanted in Dakota Territory, sure jail for a long spell if he's caught. Then there was a warning in today's mail that he might be heading this way," Micah said. "Meant to speak to you about it because I know what

close friends you and Benteen were once and thought he
might look you up—"

"You've given your reason; I'll give you an answer. It
is No," Lucas said. "Trav Benteen wasn't one of those
men. There's something else, though—"

Micah interrupted him: "I'm taking your word for it—
and handing out a warning because my job says I must . . . .
If Benteen does show up, don't give him help or shelter or
anything else. He heaped enough trouble on you in the
past. Don't let him pile on any more!"

"Don't worry," Lucas said quietly. "And if you'll let
me finish what I started to say, maybe I did notice something about one of those stick-up men, though I'm not
certain enough to swear to it in court. It's possible he may
have been a man who calls himself Cade."

Mark started violently at this. And Micah whistled, an
expressive sound in the darkness.

"There's only one man I ever heard of by that name,"
the marshal said. "Sid Cade, one of the trickiest and mean-
est gun fighters that ever lived—wanted half a dozen places
for some of the worst crimes in the book!"

"Like I said, I can't be completely sure," Lucas told him.
"Now, Micah, if you plan to cut trail on those two, I'll be

more than glad to ride along with you."

"No, you go on to the Madera House, have supper with Mark. I'll take a look along the river, see if I can come up with something," Micah said.

He mounted his deep-chested roan, then, and spurred away, past the willows toward the shallow river ford where the stagecoaches crossed to the north bank.

The Madera House was the biggest building in town, three stories high and always busy. Its lobby lamps, red plush furniture, and waxed floors dazzled Mark, walking in from the street with Lucas. It was always a big event when there was some reason to come here.

The lobby was crowded with people: army officers in their blue uniforms; wagon freighters with coiled whips; a hide-hunter leaning on his big Sharps rifle; an Indian agent with two blanketed Arapaho chiefs, feathers in their hair. Dandy Griffin, who drove the stagecoach into the territory north of the river, was busy booking passengers for tomorrow's run.

And a lean, grizzled man who, coming from the dining room, wore a fringed buckskin coat and big sombrero, said, "Lucas McCain, by glory!"

They squeezed each other's hands hard. Lucas said, "Rufe, haven't you hit town a mite early?"

"My herd's some days behind me," the other answered. "Cattle thicker than sand fleas in July, all the way down to Doan's Crossing on Red River! Going to be a shortage of cars when they hit the railroad, and I came ahead to order mine."

Then Lucas introduced Mark. "This is Rufus Dabney, son, the best trail-driver I ever knew."

"He's fooling you, boy," Dabney said. "Lucas McCain is the best man who ever brought a herd through the Nations, and you can tell everybody I said so!"

The two men talked together for a minute, agreeing that it looked like a boom year for cattlemen, prices high and the whole country clamoring for beef. Rufus Dabney said, "Lucas, you ought to be down on the trail, bringing your own cattle north."

"Everything I want is right here, Rufe: a place of my own to build up, to turn over to Mark one of these days," Lucas told him.

He and Mark went on to the washroom. Mark scrubbed diligently, using plenty of soap and paying special attention to his neck and ears, since he knew that if he didn't pass inspection Lucas would tell him to do it over again.

In the dining room they took a corner table and Lucas leaned the rifle against the wall, within easy reach. It wasn't considered good manners to wear a belt-gun in such a place, but everybody knew there were men who packed them under their coats—and among them might be a man who would like to catch Lucas McCain without that deadly rifle handy.

The table had a white cloth and gleaming silver—also napkins. Mark wasn't disturbed. Lucas had decreed the use of napkins at home often enough for him to learn how to handle them right. He had taught Mark how to eat politely too.

"Habits are hard to break, once they're set, and you might as well learn good ones right from the start," Lucas had said. "One of these days you'll be mingling with people who will judge you by such things."

Mark leaned over the hand-written bill of fare, which offered such delicacies as roast venison, bear haunch, and antelope stew. But, being a staunch cattleman, he decided on beefsteak. Lucas smiled at his choice, then ordered the same thing.

They ate without much talk. Something was bothering

Lucas, and Mark thought he knew what it was: Micah's rejection of his offer to help cut trail on the two holdup men. Lucas was wondering whether his known past friendship with Travis Benteen had influenced the marshal's decision.

There was also the fact that Lucas had not mentioned he had seen and talked to Benteen this morning, perhaps because he was hoping Benteen himself had had nothing to do with robbing Sam Bullard.

They had finished their meal and Lucas was stirring his second cup of coffee, deep in thought, when he suddenly started violently, shoved his chair back and rose quickly to his feet, with a look on his face that Mark had never seen before. Then he was plunging across the dining room toward the lobby doors—leaving his rifle behind, and it was wholly unlike him to forget it.

A woman had come in. Mark saw her stop and stiffen, hand lifting to her throat, with an expression which mixed great surprise and dismay.

Lucas reached her. He started talking. The woman still stared at him, wide-eyed. She was quite pretty, with hair the color of a young bay colt, and wore a blue dress with long puffed sleeves and a sort of high collar at her throat.

It seemed quite evident she was very upset at having encountered Lucas McCain here.

Mark stood up. He took the rifle across the room. When he reached his father's side, Lucas was speaking, "You'd have gone on through here, Susan, without letting me know?"

"I—I heard you had settled somewhere in this country, Lucas, but had forgotten the name of the town," the woman said. "I wish now I had remembered and hadn't come here at all. I don't want to talk to you. We have nothing to say to each other."

"Yes, we do," Lucas told her. "And it must be said."

Studying the woman, Mark realized it was as though he had seen her somewhere before, though he was sure that this had never happened.

"I won't listen," the woman said. "I know what you'll tell me, because I heard it all, from others, before leaving Texas. And I'm going on to Deadwood on the stage in the morning—with Madge—"

For the first time, Mark noticed a girl who was standing beside the woman, a girl of about his own age. She had dark-colored hair which fell to her shoulders, and big dark eyes which smiled at Mark as though pleading for him to smile back. There were things here which she did not understand either.

Mark returned the smile. Then the woman was looking down at him. "Good heavens, this can't be! But—yes—Margaret's eyes and chin . . . . And he's so big!"

"Mark," Lucas said, "this is your Aunt Susan."

Mark knew then why he had felt he knew her. She looked so much like the picture of his mother, which hung in Lucas' bedroom. This must be her sister.

"And your cousin, Madge," Lucas continued.

The girl smiled again. Mark bobbed his head, a little awkwardly. These were the first of his far-off relatives he had ever met.

And Lucas went on, "Susan, there's no use going to Deadwood. He isn't there. I saw him this morning."

The woman's eyes seemed to grow enormous. "He—he's here, then—in this town?"

"Probably not," Lucas said. "And I don't think there's any chance of you seeing him. Because he's on the dodge, wanted by the law."

"Oh, no!" the woman whispered.

"He has caused you enough worry and hurt," Lucas said. "You must forget him—go back home—"

"No!" Mark's Aunt Susan said again. Then she fainted, into Lucas McCain's arms.

They made their return ride to the ranch an hour or so later, under bright stars in the warm May night.

Lucas had helped the woman up to her room at the hotel, had stayed with her for some time before joining Mark again in the lobby.

It wasn't until they were stripping their horses at the corral, rubbing them down, that Lucas finally spoke: "Mark, I never did tell you much about your kinfolks. I had a reason—old troubles that were best forgotten. . . ."

Mark slung Latigo's saddle on his shoulder and took it into the barn. Lucas lighted a lantern. Mark pegged the saddle, then hung up the blanket, smoothing it out. Lucas went on, "I'll tell you now . . . or maybe you've figured things out for yourself?"

"I think I have," Mark said. "Aunt Susan is married to Trav Benteen?"

"Yes," Lucas said. "And Madge is his daughter."

He went on, "Trav sent for them to come to Deadwood and join him. That must have been before he got in trouble there. He hasn't seen either of them in more than

four years. Now they're here, and I'm afraid the holdup
tonight may indicate Trav means to hang around, somewhere close to North Fork, for a while—with Sid Cade and
the others of his bunch."

Lucas pegged his own gear. He blew out the lantern,
and they walked on to the house. There, tilting the chimney
of the oil lamp on the kitchen table, touching a match to
its wick, Lucas suddenly smiled.

"No use borrowing trouble; we'll forget all about it until
tomorrow," he said. "Brush your teeth now, use plenty of
soda and salt, then hit your bunk."

Lucas began to whistle, going to his room. He brought
back a book, settling beside the lamp with it to read for a
bit, his custom sometimes before bed.

But when Mark awoke, an hour or so later, and sent
a drowsy look into the kitchen, Lucas was not reading.
Instead, frowning intently, he was, with great care, cleaning and oiling his rifle.

4   Visitors—Three!

When you were working a ranch, there was never quite enough time for everything that had to be done. It seemed to Mark he had just closed his eyes for the second time and turned on his side when Lucas was shaking him. "Up and out, Mark. Daylight's wasting!"

Mark put on his hat first, like good cattlemen everywhere, then his breeches and boots. He went out to the bench by the kitchen door and there washed up, with a good deal of spluttering and splashing. It was barely gray dawn, the stars still visible, though dimming.

Drying himself on one of the flour sacks that the McCains saved and used as towels, he headed to the barn for before-breakfast chores. The animals had to be fed and watered first, of course, then the stalls cleaned and fresh straw spread on the floor.

The ground was damp, with a delightful cool freshness in the air. "Had a shower about an hour ago," Lucas remarked. "You'll have to work the garden this morning, Mark, before the sun bakes the ground."

He was handling the chores with his son, although some jobs were solely Mark's responsibility—such as tending the clacking hens in a pen back of the barn. And a job it was, too, considering the coyotes, bobcats, and hawks that seemed to gather from miles around to have a try at them. But, as Lucas had observed, "Eggs for breakfast and fried chicken on Sunday will be making all that work worthwhile before long!"

Mark spread grain for the chickens and had a look at half a dozen heifers which were being kept corraled for a while before being turned out with the herd. Then he split wood for the fuel box. By that time, Lucas had the stove stoked and was fixing breakfast.

The sun was still not quite up when they sat down to feather-light soda biscuits, hominy grits, and thin steaks, sliced from a side of beef in the springhouse and fried fast in a very hot skillet. There was coffee for Lucas and milk for Mark.

The chore of milking, though, was one which Mark

didn't have to tackle yet. It was easier to pick up a gallon can each week in town.

Afterwards, with the dishes finished, Mark washing and Lucas drying—they changed off every week—and the house tidied up, the two of them headed out to the barn again. There Lucas had a look at some splintered stall sideboards, kicked out by a fractious bronc he was gentling, while Mark moved slowly to the tool rack and took down the hoe with a grimace of distaste.

Lucas, watching him, said, "It's only a tool, Mark, like an axe or a saw, and a real handy one too."

"But—doggone it, Pa, if anybody sees me using it, word will get around that I'm a hoeman!" Mark protested.

He was thinking about what Cade had said yesterday: that he and Lucas were hoemen, dirt grubbers. The charge still rankled in Mark.

"If nothing worse is ever said about you, I'll be right satisfied," Lucas said. "And the quicker you get at that garden, the quicker you can put the hoe up again."

This seemed pretty good advice. Mark set to vigorously. But, as always, the garden rows seemed to stretch out, while the sun grew high and hot. And there was no use trying any short cuts or skipping any corners, because

Lucas would come to inspect the job and he might as well do it right before that happened.

Mark worked as fast as he could, with the thought that one of his friends just might happen along. It would be bad enough if the someone happened to be Micah, or Doc Harvey, or a rider from one of the ranches west of town, but it would be even worse if it happened to be one of the North Fork boys of his own age.

So keeping a wary eye on the road, and wistfully attentive to what Lucas was doing, he worked the hoe until his back began to ache. His father hammered and sawed for a bit in the barn, then went to work the bronc, with some exciting sounds from the corral.

And when somebody did come along, Mark didn't notice until the rig was in the yard—a buggy from the Gem Livery and a couple of people getting out.

They were his Aunt Susan and his cousin, Madge.

Mark stared, trying to figure what they were doing here. He saw his father appear and speak to them. Then Lucas hailed him and he went slowly to join the group, taking the hoe along because Lucas was strict about tools not being left just anywhere, but trying to make it as inconspicuous as possible.

He made his manners to Aunt Susan and said, "Hello," rather stiffly to the girl. She smiled at him, showing a dimple in her cheek. Madge's mother said something polite, her voice sounding strained. Then Lucas said, "Mark, your aunt and I have some things to talk over. Why don't you show Madge around?"

Anything was all right that meant he could let up hoeing for a while. Mark went to the barn to put the hoe back in its rack, Madge trailing along. She looked thoughtfully around. "You keep things nice here, Mark. My grandpa— he's your grandpa, too, of course—says you can tell all there is to know about a rancher just by a look at how he keeps his barn."

Mark knew his grandfather ran a big ranch in Texas. Madge started to tell him about it as they left the barn and went on to the corral, then broke off as she looked the horses over. "That light sorrel—what a beautiful pony!"

She meant Mark's own mount. He whistled Latigo over; Madge made up to him, fondling his velvety muzzle and neck. She wasn't skittish, like most girls around horses, and went on, "The pinto is nice too."

There were six horses in the corral. The pinto was a recent acquisition, thrown in as boot when Lucas traded for the

bronc he was gentling to the saddle. Back in a corner the
pinto shook his head and snorted, not a fractious sort of
animal but just a little nervous. Madge smiled, "I'd love
to try riding him! Could I?"

Mark studied her in some surprise. She wore a sort of
green suit with a jacket and fairly long skirt, also high-
buttoned shoes with red tassels at the tops. "You can't ride
in that outfit. And we don't have any sidesaddle here—"

"Don't be silly," she said. "I wouldn't dream of trying
to ride in this outfit! You must have some spare gear you
can loan me?"

As it happened, Mark did, but he thought Lucas would
veto her request. Girls just didn't put on saddle breeches
and go riding—at least not the girls he knew at the North
Fork school. To his surprise, though, when they went to
the house to check, Lucas quickly nodded in agreement.
"Sounds like a good idea. You can show her the south
pasture and the white-faces. Put your own saddle on the
pinto and use mine for Latigo, Mark. Also, you can lend
Madge your old boots."

Aunt Susan didn't object either. She and Lucas were sitting together on the front porch. Madge's mother still wore
a strained look on her pretty face and seemed to be doing

some serious thinking about something else.

Mark took the girl inside and dug out riding gear for her, then left and returned to the corral. He dabbed a loop on the pinto, pulled him to the snubbing post, and put on Latigo's saddle. When it was well-cinched, he took the rope off and mounted the horse.

As he had figured, the pinto, which hadn't been worked for several days, was full of ginger. He tried a couple of bucks and then tore around the corral, snorting, eager to run, scattering the other animals. Mark enjoyed the action. He had the edge off the pinto by the time Madge came along.

She looked considerably different, slim and handling herself with an ease which Mark found unusual. Any other girl, he thought, would have done some giggling. But Madge apparently wasn't the giggling type, at all.

Her long dark hair was pulled back in a pony-tail and tied with a bit of ribbon. She was wearing Mark's second-best boots, put aside when Lucas had given him the new hand-tooled ones last Christmas. They were Mark's greatest pride, those new boots; for a while he had been reluctant to take them off even in his bunk.

He handed her the reins. "Now, this is the right side for

mounting a horse. Take good hold on the saddle horn and put your foot in the stirrup, there. Then I'll give you a boost—"

Madge looked at him with her mouth quirking just a little. "That's good advice, Mark. There's just one thing you've left out."

"I have?" he said. "What?"

"Why, to tell me that I must be sure to face toward the front of the horse, and not his tail, when I'm in the saddle!" Madge said.

Then, disdaining any help, she swung lightly up, tapped the pinto with her heels and was off on a rush about the corral, handling the reins with a sure, deft touch, wheeling the little horse this way and that, alternating right leads and left leads, figure-eighting, taking a couple of more bucks that he still had left in him with no trouble at all.

Mark discovered his mouth was sagging open in surprise. He closed it, feeling a little ruffled. She could ride as well as he could—nearly as well, anyway—something he might have guessed, since Madge had spent some time on their grandfather's ranch. Still, she could have given him a hint about her ability before he made that speech about how to mount a horse without falling.

Madge slid the pinto to a halt and looked down at him. Her eyes were sparkling, there was color in her cheeks, she was thoroughly enjoying herself. "What are you waiting for, Mark? Saddle up your sorrel and let's go!" she said.

They rode to the house first. As they stopped by the porch rail, Mark heard his aunt say, " . . . and I must see him, Lucas! I simply must—"

Then her voice chopped off. She looked down at her hands, in her lap, which were pulling and tugging at a handkerchief.

Lucas glanced at the two of them. "Stay away from the river, Mark. And don't be gone too long. Come back in about an hour."

They wheeled off, past the irrigation ditch. Just beyond, there was a short stretch of stake-an'-rider fence, which had been on the place when the McCains acquired it. Madge sent the pinto at this, and over it, in an easy, soaring leap. So she could handle a jumper too. Mark felt tempted to follow suit with Latigo, but instead went around the fence.

Madge had stopped and was waiting for him. Mark wondered if she would comment about him failing to jump Latigo, maybe that he was scared of the fence—in which case he supposed he'd have to bite his tongue and keep quiet, since Lucas had drilled into him not to wrangle with a girl.

But instead, Madge said, "I guess it was wrong of me to take that fence. You probably don't jump your horses when they're being trained for range work?"

"That's right," Mark admitted, surprised that she should have such savvy.

"I won't do it again," Madge promised. "Now, where do we go from here?"

They rode along the irrigation ditch, but slanted away from it. Mark was mindful of Lucas' order to stay clear of the river. Madge looked toward the timber there. "I'd like to see what's yonder. But maybe I can do it later."

Mark wondered what "later" meant. "Are you and your mother—Aunt Susan—going to stay around town for a while?" he asked.

"I don't think Mamma has decided yet," Madge answered vaguely.

Then, eyes suddenly sparkling, "Let's have a race, Mark! I dare you . . . to that lone tree yonder!"

It was a distance of about half a mile. Ordinarily, Latigo

could have outrun the pinto with ease, but Madge had gotten the jump on Mark, gaining a quick early lead which
he could not cut down. She flashed past the tree—it was a
tall willow, almost in the center of the south pasture—and
won by a good half-length.

Mark felt like grumbling about her starting before he
was ready, but Madge was so delighted with her victory
that he decided not to. There was a feeling in him that
Madge Benteen didn't have an awful lot to be happy
about; and if winning a race gave her so much pleasure,
he shouldn't mind.

Anyway, there was plenty, this day, to make him feel
good. He was riding Lucas' saddle, always a treat, and
Madge was pretty good company. Maybe, like most girls,
she talked too much, he thought, but a lot that Madge said
made pretty good sense.

They had a look at the McCain cattle, the whitefaces:
Herefords. Like other Texans, Madge was loyal to longhorns and inclined to sniff, but when Mark pointed out
how much easier these were to handle and how much more
beef was on them, she had to admit that perhaps raising
purebreds instead of the half-wild longhorns might be a
very smart move.

She wanted to work some of the cattle. Mark was dubious. "That pinto hasn't been trained to cut yet, but I suppose I can help you some with Latigo—"

"You stay back!" Madge said. "I know all about cutting!"

She didn't, of course, any more than he did, but still Madge made a pretty good showing. Mark admitted as much when she had enough and reined down the tired pinto. Her features were flushed; her hair had come unbound and was flying about her face.

"You'd make a good puncher!" he exclaimed, and Madge smiled with pleasure, brushing her hair back. Then she turned to peer toward the eastern corner of the big pasture, pointing. "Mark, what is that?"

He looked, and felt the heart-squeezing moment of fright once more. It was smoke, again, curling lazily up yonder —from the grass!

This time, Madge didn't get the jump on him. He was a good hundred feet ahead of her when he jumped down and ran forward to where fire had burned a big, ragged black circle. It was smoldering, rather than burning—the grass still damp from the dawn shower—but a few lickings of flame showed here and there around the edge. Mark began to work fast at stomping them out.

After only a couple of minutes of this, he became aware that Madge was doing the same thing. Mark said, "Let me handle it!"

She tossed her head. "And maybe have it take hold and spread, before you could get it all out?"

They worked in opposite directions around the circle, met on the far side. Madge said, "Mark, that fire was started! But who would do such a thing?"

He looked around, but didn't see anything or anybody in sight. He was still cold inside. "Come on, we're going back to the house, as fast as we can travel."

"Whatever you say," she agreed, suddenly subdued.

Sid Cade had started the fire, Mark told himself, another attempt to burn the McCains out. And maybe the gunman was somewhere close by, right now, watching them, about to strike again.

5   The Crooked Box Shoe

When they arrived back at the house, Mark's Aunt Susan was already in the buggy, waiting. Madge hurried inside to change again. Mark rode on to the corral where he unsaddled Latigo, put Lucas' saddle aside—his father, he knew, would soon be using it—and transferred his own saddle to Latigo.

He went back, then, in time to hear his aunt say, "I can't do it, Lucas, and I won't!" Then Madge joined her, and good-bys were said.

"I'd like to come back sometime," she told Mark. "May I?"

"Sure, any time," Mark assured her. She was good company. He was already looking forward to riding with her again. But he was also wondering how much longer Madge would be in North Fork.

Lucas soon answered that. Looking after the buggy as it rolled away, he said, "Your Aunt Susan wouldn't take my advice, Mark, and go home. She's going to stay in North Fork awhile, hoping for a chance to see Trav Benteen."

Which meant, Mark told himself, he would probably soon be seeing both of them again. But thinking about that, and the fact they would likely land in trouble if they tried to get in touch with Benteen, could wait until later. He told hurriedly about the fire in the south pasture.

Lucas listened, brow furrowing. "You did just right, not speaking of it until those women were off the place, Mark. Any sign of the one who set the fire?"

"I didn't do much looking, Pa," Mark confessed. "Just wanted to get it out, and Madge safe back here—"

"That was right too. But you should have told Madge to return as soon as you saw the smoke."

"I don't think telling her would have done much good, even if I had thought of it. She went right along and helped me stomp the fire out." He added, "Madge was right handy at it too. She's all right—for a girl."

The furrowed lines eased a little as Lucas smiled. "You're going to discover, son, as you grow older, that women are surprisingly handy at doing a great many things a man thinks only he can handle. It sounds like your cousin is pretty smart—spunky too."

"I guess," Mark agreed. And, "I took your gear off Latigo, because I figured you'd want to saddle up and head there quick."

"You figured right," Lucas said. And Mark, hoping he would be invited to ride along, held his breath as his father turned away, toward the corral.

But Lucas stopped short, because somebody else was coming, this time from the direction of the river.

It was Micah Torrance. He looked tired, and so did his roan. The horse splashed through the irrigation ditch and moved on toward them.

Both of the McCains said quick hellos. Micah was liked a lot here. But the marshal, halting, looking down at them, did not return their welcoming smiles.

"Lucas, the pair that held up Sam Bullard last night crossed the ford to the north bank," Micah said. "I tracked them awhile, then lost their trail. One was riding a horse with a crooked box shoe—off hind hoof. I nighted over there, then headed back. And I saw that crooked box shoe again, along with some other sign, close to where a fire had been built against a big cottonwood, near the south bank

yonder, and it was on your land. . . ."

Which meant he had discovered where Trav Benteen and his bunch had been yesterday. And nobody could read sign better than Micah, unless it was Lucas.

"The rain wasn't hard enough to wash out the prints under that tree," the marshal went on. "It told a plain story. You were there, Lucas. And Mark. Also, five riders—among them the fellow whose horse has a crooked shoe. You had a talk with them."

Lucas smiled tightly. "It wasn't exactly a friendly conversation, Micah."

"Maybe not. Sid Cade one of them?"

"Yes," Lucas admitted.

"Was Benteen there too?"

"He was there," Lucas said.

"Why didn't you tell me that yesterday?"

"Several reasons. Benteen wasn't one of the pair who took Sam Bullard's money. I thought Cade might have quit him—or been forced to quit—with Benteen heading on south, and the stick-up solely Cade's doing. I'm not so sure of that now. Also, something has happened since then. . . ."

He hesitated. Micah said, "Go on!"

"Trav's wife is in North Fork, along with her daughter,

who is about Mark's age. They were heading up to Dead-wood to join Benteen. Now they're staying."

Micah frowned wearily at this news. "More trouble to come then," he said. "And some of it is liable to rub off on you, Lucas. I'm not the only one in North Fork who knows about you and Benteen having been good friends. If he shows up around here again—and it seems likely that is going to happen—don't keep it to yourself. Let me know, quick!"

"I will," Lucas promised.

"The same goes for Sid Cade," Micah said.

"If I get another look at Sid Cade, you won't be hearing about it," Lucas told him. "I'll be bringing him to you, Micah!"

Mark and his father rode to the south pasture, but not together. Lucas took the lead, with Mark staying well back.

There had been no argument about Mark going along. "As much danger leaving you here as there is in taking you with me, I suppose, if Cade started that fire and is still around," Lucas had decided. "But you stay about fifty yards back—and I mean stay there! If trouble starts, don't try to join me—remember that!"

Lucas rode again with rifle resting on saddle horn, ready for anything. He reached the ragged circle of burned grass and lifted his hand, without looking around. Mark saw his father send Razor at a slow walk completely around the circle, alternately studying the ground and everything else in sight.

Then Lucas dismounted and moved about on foot, rifle now in hand, more closely examining the ground. Presently he glanced toward Mark and signaled him on forward.

When Mark reached him, Lucas pointed toward a clear patch of sandy loam. Some hoofprints showed there. Mark bent for a close inspection. He said, "The crooked box shoe!"

"Yes. A horse ridden by either Cade or his side pardner. I don't think there's a chance in a thousand that it wasn't Cade who set the fire. They came from the direction of the river, crossed our land, probably about sunup, then headed on southward."

Mark looked toward the south. He saw a wide, dusty plain, which looked flat and smooth, but wasn't. Rather, it was crosshatched by numerous gullies, draws, arroyos, and even shallow canyons. Several creeks flowed there, slanting on eastward to join the river.

Against the southern horizon a long line of ragged-topped mesas showed, brown and reddish and black in the bright sun. Mark had been out on the plain, for there were the bed-grounds used by the Texas herds, where they were held before being brought on through. Lucas had taken him for visits to the cattle camps last summer.

He had never been as far south as the mesas, but had always hoped for the day when he could see what was there, and beyond them.

"You think maybe those two were heading to join Benteen and the others of that bunch?" Mark ventured.

Lucas took another look at the hoofprints and nodded. Then he turned to Razor and checked the black's cinch, pulling it a little tighter.

This meant he was planning to follow where those hoofprints led. Mark waited, holding his breath again. Lucas might decide to tell him to go visit in North Fork for a while. However, that could be dangerous, too, since there was no telling where Sid Cade might be.

Lucas must have taken this into account. At last he glanced to Mark and nodded. "The same as before, son. Stay behind me, about the same distance. If there's trouble, don't get involved. We might have a ride for nothing; but, on the other hand, it seems likely they wouldn't head too far south before making camp."

He led out, easy and erect in the saddle, as always. Mark waited. Presently Lucas glanced around, with the slight lift of his rein hand. Mark nudged Latigo and followed him.

The warmth and sunshine held until sometime after noon, when clouds began to fill the sky and a wind started to blow from the north. Maybe there would be more showers.

Lucas maintained an easy range pace, a little faster than a walk, but not quite a trot, which covered ground at a surprising rate of speed. He would dip into an arroyo, and Mark would stop, waiting until his father appeared again, indicating it was clear there, no danger, when Mark would go on again.

He was closely following Razor's tracks and every now and then had a glimpse of the crooked box shoe, indicating how sharply Lucas' attention was on the trail of those two they were seeking.

Latigo did not like such slow going and began to snort, tossing his head, jerking hard on the reins, to show he had run in him and wanted to use it.

"Listen, it's hard on me too," Mark informed the horse. A lonesome business, this riding alone, when he would much rather be alongside his father.

After quite a while, he looked back. They had covered at least a dozen miles, and the line of timber at the river was a thin band of green now against the northern horizon. There was no rain yet, but the day had turned gray and murky.

The buttes ahead were now no more than half a dozen miles away. Mark looked toward the break in them, off at his right, westward, where the cattle were trailed down to the bed-grounds; but there was no sign of any herd using that trail yet.

Mark suddenly realized he hadn't seen the mark of the crooked box shoe for some time. They were now working along the base of a rise where the ground was hard and gravelly and where no tracks showed.

Lucas stopped and dismounted, with a gesture which told Mark to come on and join him. Mark did so. Lucas said, pointing, "Put the horses over there."

It was a dip in the land, nearby, where some stunted willows showed. Mark led both animals to it, loosened cinches and removed bits so they could rest comfortably, made sure they were well-tied, and hurried back to rejoin his father.

Lucas was working his way up the rise afoot. Mark started to join him. He saw his father hit the dirt and then move on, pulling himself along with his elbows, the rifle out before him, and realized Lucas wanted a look from the top of the rise without himself being observed. Mark hit the dirt also, staying behind him.

Lucas reached the crest of what was actually a ridge that lifted about fifty feet above the general level of the plain. He took a long look forward while Mark waited. Then Lucas glanced around.

"A creek ahead," he reported in a low voice. "I had a feeling they'd be there, for sure, but can't see anything. You come and take a look, Mark."

Wriggling on forward, slanting a little away from Lucas, Mark saw the creek. It was about half a mile on southward, with a bordering line of willows and aspens, trees that were thick in some spots, thin in others.

He didn't see any sign of the men they were seeking either, no telltale wisp of smoke from a campfire, no horses, no movement anywhere.

"Well, I could have figured it wrong," Lucas remarked.

"They could have gone on up into the mesa country, where we sure aren't going to follow them. But there's also the chance I figured it right. . . ."

He suddenly shifted position, looking off toward the west, deliberately raising himself a little. A gun cracked instantly, a bullet whining somewhere over Mark's head.

Lucas swung his rifle and fired in return. Mark, who was as close to the ground as he could get, saw a rider appear below the ridge, heading fast toward the creek, twisting in his saddle to trigger more bullets. He was using a handgun.

Lucas fired again, kicking dirt just ahead of the running horse, which meant he could knock the man out of his saddle if he wanted to.

Some more shooting began, by a couple of men who had appeared, afoot, this side of one of those thick clusters of trees. They were yelling and also using handguns, but the distance was so great, of course, that the chance of scoring a hit was pretty remote.

A group of four horses appeared, one man riding and leading the others, splashing along in the creek. The horses had been carefully hidden. So had the camp site picked by Trav Benteen for his men. Mark had a glimpse of Benteen himself, his big figure unmistakable.

Lucas studied the scene for a moment, then went to work. It took only three bullets from his rifle to drive back to cover those two on this side of the creek, and he could have scored hits on them also.

They went in among the trees and did a bit more shooting, kicking up some dust on the downward slope of the ridge, but well off to the left.

Benteen must have realized he was at a bad disadvantage: no chance of getting at Lucas, all of his men too vulnerable. Lucas emphasized this by putting a bullet fairly close to Benteen himself, even though he was over on the creek's south bank.

The others splashed across to join him. Then they were all mounting up and hurriedly pulling out, a move which must have galled Benteen—the necessity to run from the rifle.

He and his bunch headed away toward the south and west. Benteen was at the head of the single file of riders. Sid Cade brought up the rear; he was easily recognizable too. Mark saw Cade turn to yell something and felt the full force of his anger, even at this distance.

Lucas used three more bullets, placing them close to the horsemen, making them move faster. Then he stood up.

"Hoped to work right up to them without being spotted," he commented, "but Trav handled it smart, planting a man this side of the creek to keep watch."

Mark rose also. He began to collect the ejected cartridge cases.

"A fellow who had an itchy trigger finger," Lucas went on. "A good thing for us he did."

But Lucas had been smart also, figuring the possibility of a gunman being planted there, keeping watch. Even if the fellow hadn't had an itchy trigger finger, Mark thought, Lucas would, through some other means, have forced him to betray himself.

"We'll head for home now," Lucas continued. "All of our riding wasn't wasted. We learned something."

Something he had hoped that he wouldn't find out: that Cade was still one of Benteen's bunch. This made Trav Benteen also guilty of the holdup last night, even though he himself hadn't been there.

"Maybe they'll just keep on, into the mesas and on south," Mark suggested hopefully. "Maybe this is the last time we'll see them."

"I wish I could believe that, but I can't," Lucas said, shaking his head. "Not with the Texas herds due soon, when the owners will be selling their cattle and carrying big rolls of cash. There'll be rich pickings then for men like Benteen and Cade. I'm afraid they'll still be around, to cause more trouble for everybody."

But especially, it seemed probable, for the McCains.

They were about halfway back to the ranch, moving more briskly and thinking of evening chores to be done there, when a lone horseman appeared before them on the plain.

He was leading a pack mule with a heavy load, and as he came closer Mark discovered he was the Texan met last night at the Madera House, Rufus Dabney. There was a genial "Howdy!" as he paused for a moment. And, "I'm heading back to join my boys, taking along the fixings for a big feed on the last night out. Figure to meet up with them tomorrow or the next day."

"Rufe, I wish you weren't riding alone," Lucas said, his face grave. "The men who hit Sam Bullard last night are on the loose, close by. We had a look at them a while ago."

The big Texan laughed. "Lucas, are you trying to make me spooky?"

"If you're packing along anything else—like pay for your crew, for instance—I wish you'd turn back and get at least a couple of good gun-handlers to ride with you," Lucas said.

It seemed to Mark that the man's eyes flickered for a moment, as though evading Lucas' grave scrutiny. Then he snorted, shaking out his reins. "It'll be a cold day in August when Rufe Dabney goes begging help from anybody! Come see me, Lucas, when I make camp, and bring your boy along. I got some tall tales to tell him."

He moved on. Lucas looked after him for several minutes.

Then, "Mark, never get so proud and stubborn that you'll ignore a warning of danger. Now, let's hustle along. Those chores are waiting."

6   Runaway!

The rain held off until night, when there was a brisk downpour. But at dawn all the clouds were gone, with the promise of another hot day.

Before Lucas' hand could touch Mark's shoulder, he was up and hurrying through the chores, but not because he was impatient to finish hoeing the garden again. That wouldn't be required of him today.

This was Saturday, when Lucas hitched up the buckboard as soon as everything was squared away, to drive in to North Fork. The reason was to do the buying of supplies, staple groceries for the following week and whatever items might be needed for working the ranch. But there was even more to such town visits.

Saturday was when everybody in the back country came to North Fork, with a chance to swap news, visit around, renew old friendships. Like most of the others, the McCains generally got there before noon and didn't head back until dark.

Lucas enjoyed such layoffs from work as much as Mark did. So it came as a big surprise when, after breakfast dishes were put away and it was time to hitch up, Lucas said, "Mark, I think I'll let you handle the town business by yourself this week. I've got something that has to be done by me alone, and no need for you to miss the trip just because I can't go."

It didn't take much effort for Mark to figure out just what the "something" was that Lucas had in mind. He was going to hunt for Sid Cade and Travis Benteen again. Lucas had been up several times during the night; Mark had heard him pacing back and forth in the kitchen. And twice Lucas had stepped outside, to be gone for some time, possibly to look around in case they should strike back.

Lucas must have decided then to try for their trail again. And even the prospect of driving the buckboard to town alone, which had never happened before, wasn't enough to stifle Mark's wish that he might be allowed to go along.

However, he didn't beg for that. Once Lucas reached a decision, it stood, unless a very good reason could be advanced for changing it. And Mark knew he couldn't offer any reason which would impel Lucas to change his mind this time. So he went along to the barn and began to hitch the placid pair of team horses to the buckboard.

Lucas lent a hand, though Mark was almost tall enough to fit the harness on unaided. Then they returned to the house to check supplies and make up a list of things to be bought, not only flour and salt and sugar, lard, dried apples, canned tomatoes, and all the things needed to keep them eating well, but another list of the items, also, which were constantly required for running the ranch.

"Better get a box of small staples for fence mending," Lucas said. "Then stop at Wayland's Feed Barn and ask him to load on about four blocks of sulphur salt for the cattle. We'll set them out on Monday."

"There's still half a sack of feed for the chickens. We can put off getting more for them until next week," Mark said. "But the oat bin is getting a little bit low. Our horses sure eat a lot!"

"We work them a lot," Lucas said. "Tell Wayland to put on two sacks and we'll fill the bin."

He added up everything, produced his purse and counted money from it. With a smile, he commented, "Looks like there'll be enough here for a sack of stick candy and some jawbreakers too!"

Mark snorted inwardly. Once upon a time, when he was younger, a trip to town had been exciting mostly because it meant candy for him. But he figured that he was now getting too old for that.

Lucas, he thought, treated him part of the time like he was nearly grown-up, and part of the time like he was still a kid. Mark didn't much mind. He had observed that all adults had the same trouble—and he wasn't right sure himself just what he was, maybe in a sort of in-between state that he would emerge from one of these days without even knowing it was happening.

They returned to the buckboard, where Mark climbed up to the seat and took hold of the reins. Lucas, studying him, said then, "Don't stay in town too late, son. And if you get home, find I'm not here—"

But he caught himself, thought a moment, and shook his head. "No. I'm not going to give any orders. I know well enough you'll handle all the night chores, if necessary, without having to be told—also, that you'll do your best to stay out of trouble."

He stepped back. "Have a good trip. Enjoy yourself."

It wasn't until he was well along the road, in the day's bright sunlight, that Mark realized this day was a sort of milestone for him, being allowed to make the trip to town alone in the buckboard, being allowed to spend the money that would carry them through the following week.

He held the team to a steady trot. Other rigs appeared on the road, some with whole families in them, all bound for North Fork too—and Lucas must have figured there wasn't much that could happen to him on this day, with so many people around.

Mark exchanged greetings with them. He couldn't help but notice the envious looks from boys his own age, fellows he went to school with; also, he couldn't help feeling pretty good about it, though with the sobering thought that he probably wouldn't have another chance like this very soon.

He was on the main street in town a little before noon, hunting for and finding a space at the hitch-rail in front of Hattie Denton's general store. Mark eased the harness on the horses and put on their nose bags. Then he had a look around.

North Fork wasn't a very big town, but growing all the time. It had started as just one street, running south from the river. Now there were three cross streets, each with a scattering of houses.

All of the business was on Main Street, most of its frame buildings with false fronts to make them look taller. There was one brick building, two stories high, Mr. Hamilton's bank.

Nearly everybody spoke to Mark, and he had to explain constantly that Lucas wasn't along, wasn't ill either. He had a glimpse of Micah, but the marshal seemed to be in a hurry, worried about something, and didn't speak to him.

Mark walked along one side of the street and back the other. He went into the store and made his purchases there, counting out the money to pay for them, double-checking his change. Some people put everything on a bill and paid when they could, but the McCains didn't mean to go into debt and paid cash for everything.

Hattie Denton's nephew, one of Mark's closest friends, helped him carry the purchases out and stow them in the buckboard's bed. His name was Norbert, but anybody his own age who called him that was in for a fight, whereas if you called him Butch everything was all right.

Mark sat on the seat and ate some cold beef and biscuits he had brought along, meanwhile watching the street.

There was always something exciting to see in town on a Saturday. Some cavalrymen from Fort Badger, fifty miles westward along the river, on weekend leave, clattered past. The mail coach from the south arrived, its six-horse team galloping, stirring up a lot of dust.

Passengers streamed from the coach into the Madera House for a hurried lunch. Saturday in town was something to look forward to all week.

Mark moved on to Jensen's Hardware for his purchases there, then drove down to Wayland's Feed Barn.

His business at Wayland's completed, he walked over to a corral behind it. The corral belonged to a horse dealer who held an auction every Saturday afternoon; there on one never-to-be-forgotten such day Lucas had successfully bid for Latigo.

A few people had already gathered, though the auction wouldn't start until about three. Mark had a look through the poles at the milling horses, with a sharp eye for blood-lines and possible defects. Then he heard someone call his name, looked around and saw Madge Benteen scrambling down from where she was perched on the top rail.

She wore blue jeans, with the shelf-creases still showing, a new flannel shirt and red-calf boots, the jeans stuffed in so that the pull-on loops would show. Her black hair was now in two long pigtails, with yellow ribbons braided in them.

"Gosh, Mark, I'm sure glad to see you!" she exclaimed. "It's so lonesome here, not knowing anybody yet."

Madge looked toward the horses then, eyes shining. "Look at the blue roan mare! Isn't she beautiful? I wonder if maybe I could buy her? I've got about twenty dollars of my own—"

Mark shook his head. The blue roan, a sleek young animal, would be bid in for a lot more than twenty dollars. He said, "Let's go sit in the buckboard. I've got some candy. You can have a stick, if you like."

He hadn't been able to resist telling the clerk at the store to add the sack of candy to his purchases.

Madge walked around in front of the feed barn with him. They climbed up to the buckboard seat and sat together, chewing on the peppermint sticks. Madge told him that she and her mother were still staying at the hotel, that she had bought her new gear only this morning.

"Mamma fussed at me because I'm such a tomboy," Madge confessed. "But I wear clothes like these all the time in Texas, can't seem to get used to dresses."

Then, with no warning, she said, "Mark, I heard about the talk she had with Uncle Lucas, how both of you saw my father. Tell me about him, everything you can remember. Please!"

Mark hesitated for a moment, but it didn't seem that answering her could cause any harm. He told the girl all he remembered of Travis Benteen, from their meeting at the river. He didn't tell about Sid Cade, or the others.

Madge's hands were clasped tightly together when he finished. "You know where he is now," she said. It was a statement, not a question.

Mark said, "Well, not exactly—"

"I want you to take me to him!" Madge said.

"Take you!"

"Wait!" Madge said. "I know you'll say that you won't do it, or can't. But listen to me for just a second!"

She looked away from him then, moistening her lips, seeming to clasp her hands together even more tightly. "Mark, do you remember anything about your mother?"

"A—a little," he replied, with the queer, tingly sort of lost feeling that came to him whenever the lovely, gentle-eyed lady of the picture in Lucas' bedroom was mentioned.

Lucas did not speak of her much, though Mark knew

she was always in Lucas' thoughts. His father had said, "She was taken away from us, son. No use trying to figure why; maybe she was too good for this world. Such things happen. We have to learn to live with them—and to make of ourselves all she hoped we would be."

"You must miss her dreadfully. Everybody does," Madge said. "And I miss my father the same way! I—I've only seen him twice that I remember, and then only for a day or so. I've waited so long, Mark, and I want to see him again. Take me to him. Please!"

There were tears in her eyes. He felt his own eyes smart a little.

Madge hurried on, "Mamma can't go to him—not yet. The marshal here talked to her last night and warned that she was going to be watched. But who would notice what I do? I could come out to the ranch, Mark, and you could take me to my father!"

"But I can't!" Mark said. "Because I don't know where he is, not really. Somewhere south of town, but that's all."

With those four men, including Sid Cade, all of them being hunted by the law. And it made him shiver inwardly to think of encountering Sid Cade again, especially with Madge along.

Mark wondered how much she knew of what her father was, what he had done, and hoped Madge didn't know the full story. Not, he supposed, that it would make any particular difference about how she felt for him, and that was right, but he didn't mean to be the one to tell her if she didn't know.

"It can't be done," Mark repeated. "You've got to forget about trying such a thing, Madge, and wait until he can come to you."

Which might be never. Or, if they did meet, jail bars were likely to be between them when it happened.

"I can't wait," Madge said, brushing away a couple of tears which had slid down onto her cheeks. "Somewhere south of town, you said . . . . If you won't take me to him, Mark, I'll go and hunt for my father myself!"

It took quite a while for him to talk her out of that notion, and Mark wasn't sure he had really done so, though Madge at last agreed to wait a little while, at least until he could talk to Lucas about it.

Mark drove her to the Madera House, where he got out and went in to say hello to his Aunt Susan, who looked red-eyed and tired, but who insisted that he visit for a while, with talk about his relatives in Texas.

After that there wasn't much reason for him to stay in town any longer, especially as Lucas was constantly in his thoughts. He wondered whether he would find his father at the ranch when he returned.

However, he made time to call on Mrs. Harvey, the doctor's wife, and to talk to her about the mysteries of baking a cake.

Finally he headed the buckboard home, pushing the team considerably faster than on the morning trip to town, the horses' hoofs clop-clopping briskly in the road dust, flocks of meadow larks wheeling up out of the high grass on either side as he passed, the land north of the river golden in the late afternoon sunshine.

When Mark wheeled the rig into the yard between house and barn, the silence there told him Lucas had not yet come back.

The horses left in the corral crowded against the poles, nickering eagerly. Latigo, with much fretful head-tossing, showed how displeased he was at having been penned up all day.

Mark unharnessed, first, and rubbed down the team. Then he tended the stock, spreading hay and grain and water. After that he emptied the sacks of oats into the barn bin, filling it, and finally unloaded the buckboard, sorting out the food items, carrying them into the kitchen.

Lucas had left a pot of stew simmering on the stove, a pan of biscuits in the warming rack, but Mark did not feel like eating. He went out again to dip a bucket in the irrigation ditch and fill the wash barrel. He lugged in another bucket, stoked the stove, and set the bucket on to boil; later it would be put aside to cool, the water finally poured into the drinking keg where it would filter down through charcoal. Lucas was strict about not drinking anything else.

After that there wasn't anything particularly pressing that needed to be done. It was now early twilight, stars beginning to speckle a cloudless sky and a pleasant breeze blowing. The best time of the day, Lucas often said, when they would sit on the front porch, supper done, maybe talk a little but mostly just stay quiet, letting their tired muscles relax.

Far off, a coyote quavered its lonesome call and an owl hooted drowsily. Mark kept busy. He chopped wood and filled the fuel box to overflowing.

He told himself he wasn't scared, wasn't going to get scared. It was foolish to worry. There wasn't a man anywhere better able to take care of himself, under any circumstances, than Lucas McCain.

Still, no getting away from it, he did have a scary feeling, night coming on and his father not here. The house seemed awfully empty and silent, no matter how much racket he made moving about.

Then there was a sudden clatter of hoofbeats and he ran out to welcome Lucas back, to tell him all the chores were done and they could sit right down and eat.

But it wasn't Lucas that he saw—it was Madge Benteen, sitting a big, rawboned *grulla* with angry-looking eyes which was fighting its bit, dancing around in a nervous circle as she held him in check. Madge had more strength in her hands than Mark would have guessed.

He could only stare at her in complete amazement, the words bursting from him. "What are you doing here? And where did you get that horse?"

The brand on its flank was plainly visible: Bar T. That was a big stock outfit westward along the river. The *grulla* bore a double-cinched Texas saddle with stirrups set far too long for Madge; she had to grip tightly with her knees to stay on.

"I took it off a hitch-rail in town," Madge said. And,

"Listen, there's talk on the streets, a lot of excitement over something that happened. I heard part of the talk, about Uncle Lucas being seen south of here this afternoon, down toward those mesas. He went there to meet my father, didn't he?"

The enormity of what she had done staggered Mark. Taking a horse belonging to somebody else, without a by-your-leave, was about the worst thing that anybody could do.

He said, "Get down. That horse has got to go right back where you picked it up!"

With hope that nobody had yet noticed it was gone, though this seemed unlikely, Mark went at the *grulla*, trying to grab its headstall. But Madge pulled the horse away, beyond his reach.

"No!" she cried. "I'm going to find them—came by here only so you could tell Mamma where I've gone, in case I can't come back. Say I'm sorry if I cause her any worry, but it'll be all right once I'm with him—"

She gave the *grulla* a rein-cut and was gone, heading off toward the south at a driving run.

Mark looked after her for a moment. Even in that brief space of time the twilight swallowed her up.

Then he was racing for the barn to grab his saddle, duck into the corral and slap it on Latigo. He had to go after the girl, stop her before she found herself in even worse trouble than she was in already.

7   Trouble in North Fork

Later in the summer there would be longer twilights, but at this season they were pretty brief, night following swiftly. Before Mark spurred away from the house, heading south, it was nearly full dark. And a thick sort of darkness too. There would be a moon, about a quarter full, but it wouldn't rise for several hours yet.

He let Latigo run all out for a while, over country that he knew pretty well. There was hope in Mark that he could overhaul Madge fairly quickly.

But he didn't overhaul her and found that he couldn't even track the *grulla* by sound. Then, after a bit, Mark had to slow Latigo down. There was danger of the pony stepping into a prairie dog hole or going over the rim of some arroyo hidden in the darkness.

As he continued to ride along, Mark thought about what

Madge had done—with anger at first; this, however, ebbed quickly as he remembered the intensity of the girl's longing to be with her father.

She had behaved pretty foolishly, of course, but Mark thought of how he would behave if Lucas was yonder in the darkness, in trouble, and knew it wasn't his place to find fault with her.

Also, he had to save all of his energy for heading the girl off and bringing her back—if he could.

He continued to head due south, with a backward look every now and then to take a bearing on the north star. It was one of a stockman's primary duties, Lucas had once said, to know all the stars, especially for trail work. Mark had learned them pretty well.

Time stretched out. After a while he had no idea how long it had been since he had left the ranch, but it seemed like hours; he must be at least halfway toward the mesas.

Then, from somewhere far off in the night, a faint cry. Instantly Mark halted Latigo. "Hello!" he called back, "Where are you?"

The faint cry came again. Mark shouted, "Stay put! I'm coming!"

It was off to his left, eastward. He guided Latigo in that

direction. The pony was beginning to tire, also turning a little spooky because Mark, of course, had seldom done any riding at night.

He sent out a couple of more hails, with Madge's answering calls guiding him, and at last the dim silhouette of her horse appeared. The *grulla* whinnied fearfully and tried to bolt. Mark sent Latigo at it, leaned forward and managed to gain a hold on the reins. He snugged the horse down.

Madge was some distance away and now came limping toward him. She said fretfully, "He somersaulted and threw me—was too tired to bolt but kept shying away every time I tried to catch him again."

Mark dismounted, still keeping a tight hold on the *grulla's* reins, and ran a hand over the horse. Muscles quivered under his palm. "He's nearly worn out. You must have had him running all the way."

"I was in a hurry," Madge said. "I still am. And he isn't too worn out. Now you've caught him for me, I'll be going on."

Mark snorted at this. "Listen, we're going to rest both of them a bit, then we're heading back."

"We are not!" Madge cried. "You can do as you please, but I'm going to keep on until I find my father!"

Mark did not bother to answer. He had already learned that girls could get strange notions at times, and there was simply no use arguing about them. Using the *grulla's* reins, he managed to fashion a front-hobble which would hold the horse. Then he started casting about in the dark, hunting something that would burn.

He always carried a couple of sulphur matches in his pocket, wrapped in a twist of oilcloth, for emergency use only. This seemed enough of an emergency to warrant using one of them. A fire wasn't needed for warmth, but its light could help.

Presently it was blazing and Madge was sitting beside it. She had been shaken up when the *grulla* somersaulted, and bruised some, but was not otherwise hurt.

"I mean to go on," Madge said, "if I have to walk!"

Mark still didn't bother to answer her. By the stars, it was earlier than he had figured. Maybe with luck he could get her back to North Fork before her mother even noticed she was gone.

Madge turned to pleading. "Why don't you understand, Mark, and help me?"

"I do understand," Mark said. "And the best way I can help is to take you back. Your father doesn't want you with him, Madge. Where Trav Benteen is, the things he's doing, you'd not only be in the way, but in danger—"

He caught himself, with the feeling he had said too much.

Madge said, "You ought to call him Uncle Trav. Because he is your uncle, just as your father is mine."

Thinking of Trav Benteen as his uncle would take some getting used to, Mark thought.

Then the girl went on, quietly, "If you're trying to tell me he is an outlaw, I already know that. And if I have to be an outlaw, too, I will, just so I can be with him—"

Mark didn't have to comment on this. Because just then a scattering of gunshots sounded out in the darkness. Fairly far away, he thought, walking off a little in the direction from which they had come, listening hard but not hearing any more shots.

Mark was trying not to be fearful and was succeeding fairly well, though he couldn't keep down an awfully lonely feeling. There was the thick darkness, a wind that was rustling the brush, those gunshots. . . .

This was one of the moments when Mark didn't feel nearly as grown-up as he sometimes hoped he was.

He looked around at Madge, telling himself she had to

go back to North Fork with no more argument. At least, Mark told himself this, but he wasn't at all certain he could make the girl who had handled that big mouse-colored horse do anything.

Then there was a hail out in the night: "Hello, the fire! Who's there?" and Mark felt a tremendous surge of relief. Because what he heard was the voice of Lucas McCain.

When Lucas came riding up to the fire, he was not alone. Another horse, on a lead rope, trailed him. Sitting its saddle was a man, wearing a sullen, hangdog look, whose hands were tied together and also tied to his saddle horn. Mark recognized him as one of Benteen's bunch.

Lucas swung down. He spoke forcefully. "What are you two doing out here?"

Mark started to explain, with the intent of making it as easy on Madge as he could, but she cut in on him. Madge, it was evident, had no intent of letting anybody apologize for her. "I've got to find my father, Uncle Lucas. I've simply got to!"

Lucas studied her, features softening. "This isn't the way to do it, Madge. He wants to see you as badly as you want to see him—keep thinking about that and it may ease the way you feel, a little. I'll do the best I can to bring you two together—and with your mother there too. That's a promise. But right now you have to go back to North Fork."

She couldn't argue with him. Madge turned and walked off a little way by herself. She stood looking toward the south. The man whose hands were tied sent a curious glance at her. He said, "So that's Benteen's kid. Trav will sure be interested when he finds out she's so close!"

Lucas went to take a look at the *grulla*. Mark went with him and said, low-voiced, "When she rushed off like that, I felt the only thing I could do was to follow her."

"Of course," Lucas said. Then he shook his head. "That girl and her mother! I hoped to end their worries about Trav Benteen tonight, even if I had to heap another kind of grief on their heads."

He did not explain. Mark glanced toward the prisoner. "Isn't that the same one who was the lookout yesterday?"

Lucas nodded. "His name is Jeter. He was doing the same job today, posted about a mile from their camp, which they moved west, toward the headwaters of that creek we saw. All five of them there, so I knew you wouldn't be in any danger at the ranch. I hoped to work in close, wait until dark, make an effort to take them—"

Himself alone, against five outlaws, but Lucas obviously hadn't figured the odds were too great, as long as he had the rifle.

"I tried to get around Jeter, but he spotted me, yelled and cut loose," Lucas went on. "I had no choice but to grab him. The range was too long, with the darkness, for me to try for the others, and no chance then, of course, of getting close. Only one thing to do—back off and start hauling that one along to Micah."

"I heard some shooting," Mark said.

"Yes. They chased us for a bit, with wild shooting. I'm pretty sure they've given up now."

Then, "Mark, put a lead-rope on this horse and dally it around your saddle horn. We're not going to take any chance of Madge cutting off on her own again. Soon as you're ready, we'll start riding."

It was about two hours later when they came up to the outskirts of the town, the lights of which had been twinkling before them for some time. Also, they had been hearing a growing uproar of sound.

Madge and Mark were riding in front, with very little talk between them. The girl seemed tired, lost in her worried thoughts. Lucas and his prisoner trailed them. Now, at Lucas' low hail, Mark stopped. His father came alongside him.

"Take her on behind you and turn the *grulla* loose," Lucas directed. "Somebody will find him in the morning, see he gets back to Bar T, and we'll just have to hope that no one saw Madge take the horse."

Then he looked ahead. "Unusual for so many to be up this late, even on a Saturday. And I wonder what the reason is for all that yelling."

Mark remembered Madge had said there was excitement in the town. But she hadn't known the reason.

"Mark, cut away and go in along Prairie Street," Lucas said. That was the first cross street this side of the river. "Let Madge off at the hotel. I'll go by way of Cheyenne Street and deliver this fellow to Micah. You come along to his office and join me there. Then we'll go on home together."

The man whose hands were tied muttered, "You're wasting your time, McCain. Benteen will see to it I don't stay long in any cracker-box jail!"

"Keep quiet, Jeter," Lucas said. And, "Get going, Mark. I'll see you later."

All of the excitement, the hullabaloo and yelling, seemed to be taking place south along Main Street. The area near the Madera House was deserted.

Madge had been riding behind Mark, with her arms about him so she wouldn't fall off. She said in a low voice, "I'm real sorry, all the trouble I put you to."

"That's all right," Mark told her gruffly. "Just don't do it again, Madge, please!"

"I won't," she said. "I know I made a bad mistake, taking that horse, and the blame would have been on you and Uncle Lucas, as much as on me, because we're related. I won't do anything like that again."

Mark dismounted, then, and helped her down. Madge put her hand over his, with a hard squeeze. She turned and ran up the steps, across the hotel porch, in through the lobby doors.

He looked after her, realizing Madge hadn't promised much, only that she wouldn't help herself to any more horses from North Fork hitch-rails.

She had not promised that she would not make another effort to find her father, some other way, and Mark wondered what plan might be stirring in her head now to bring that about. He had a feeling Madge was going to cause more trouble for himself and Lucas.

An outburst of shouting down the street turned his attention in that direction. A crowd was milling around there, beyond Micah's office, and the sound being made by that crowd had an ugly, growling undertone in it.

A horse, hard-driven, came up the street. Its rider spun his mount around, near Latigo, with a yell. He wore ragged range gear which looked as though he hadn't taken it off in a month. His straggly beard made him look as though he hadn't shaved in that long either.

Double-cinched saddle, high-crowned hat, big rowels on his spurs—Mark had seen this kind before. This was a Texas trail hand. The first of the great herds must have arrived.

A man came out on the hotel porch, one who was only a little less ragged, but equally as tough-looking. "What do you want, Cash?" he demanded.

"Thought you'd like to know the tin-star here has got one of the bunch that hit the boss," the man on horseback said. "And—tie this if you can—it was Lucas McCain who brought him in!"

"Why come and tell me?" the man on the porch snapped. "You've got plenty of the boys with you—plenty of help from this town, too, looks like. Take that joker out and string him up. . . . And you know what to do with McCain and the law if they try to get in your way!"

"Just wanted to check," the one on horseback said, turning his mount to start back. But he hesitated. "How about Rufe? Any change?"

"Not much. We've got him in bed here. The town doc says he's in no particular danger—won't soon be getting over the beating those scuts handed him, though. He's bruised all over."

It all seemed clear enough to Mark. They were talking about Rufus Dabney. What Lucas had feared must have happened. Benteen's bunch had stopped the big cattleman somewhere along the trail and he had taken a bad beating from them.

More, most of Dabney's trail crew must be in North Fork. They were in an angry mood. They meant to seize the outlaw Lucas had brought in.

Mark heeled Latigo down Main Street also. But, half a block short of Micah's office, he turned aside, stopped and made his tie at a hitch-rail. Lucas wouldn't want him involved in any way with that angry, gathering mob. At the same time, though, Mark itched to see what was going on—and if Lucas needed any help that he could give, he didn't mean to stand still.

The crowd was just beyond the next corner, plainly visible. It looked as though every lamp in town was lighted and shining on the street. And some of the men yonder had lanterns.

They seemed to be just surging back and forth, from one side of the street to the other, with a lot of yelling, as though working themselves up. Mark saw one who had a coil of rope which he brandished over his head, shouting for the rest to come along and help him use it. The looks on their faces, the noises they were making—they were behaving more like animals than men.

Then Mark saw someone he recognized, a rather mousy and quiet little fellow named Smithers who ran a saddle shop. He had climbed up in a wagon bed on the far side of the street and was shouting for attention.

"Listen to me!" Smithers cried, waving his arms. "All of you—wait a minute and listen!"

They quieted down somewhat, surging about the wagon, looking up to him.

"First it was Sam Bullard, and now Rufus Dabney," Smithers shouted. "Both of them cut down and robbed—by the same bunch, a trigger-happy gang of killers headed up by Trav Benteen!"

"Yeah! With Lucas McCain mixed up in it, both times —don't forget that!" somebody shouted.

"And him Benteen's saddle-pardner once!" another man called out.

Mark clenched his fists indignantly at this slur against his father.

"We can let that go until later," Smithers said. "Right now, we've got to think about something else—what is liable to happen to North Fork if we don't take some action—right now!"

He paused, looking around. The man had their full attention. "I'll tell you what will happen," he continued. "This isn't the only town along the river. Unless we do something right away to wipe out that bunch of thieves, show the cattlemen they can come here without fear of being robbed, they'll take their herds somewhere else! And before this summer is over, North Fork will be a ghost town. We'll all have to pull up stakes, leave everything we have here, and move!"

A roar went up at that. The crowd began to surge toward Micah's office. Smithers pointed in that direction.

"One of them is sitting over there in the jail right now—let's take him!"

The man with the coil of rope was out in front.

That was when Micah Torrance emerged from his office, moved across the walk, and stopped just short of stepping down into the street. Right behind him was Lucas, the rifle under his arm with its muzzle slanting down. His expression was grim.

Micah lifted his hands. Both of them were empty. His gun was still in its holster. "You men!" he called. "Stop that yelling and get off the street!"

Jeers answered him. Smithers shouted, "We want your prisoner, Micah! Turn him over to us!"

"No!" Micah roared. "As long as I wear this badge, he stays in his cell, waiting for a fair trial—"

A gun barked somewhere in among the crowd. Mark did not see who fired it. But, catching his breath, he did see Micah, hit hard, spin around and fall against a post, clutching his right arm as he slid on down, falling on his side on the walk.

It was as though the shot had triggered the whole mob into instant action. With a thunderous roar it surged on forward, men shoving, pushing, jostling in their eagerness to be in the front rank of those wanting to get at Micah's prisoner.

Lucas took two long steps into the street and turned to face them directly—one man against at least a hundred, and the nearest of them less than fifty feet away.

8   A Win and a Loss

Lucas wasted no time in trying to plead or argue with the wildly clamoring men who were bearing down on him. The rifle seemed to spin up into waist-level firing position as though it were part of him; it began to spit lead in swift, stuttering roars, and again Lucas' right hand was working faster than the eye could follow its movements.

He was not firing over the heads of these people, though, as he had done when Sid Cade faced him. Rather, he was firing just short of the feet of those who were foremost in the mob, spraying fire which swept the street from one side to the other, dirt spouting up like fat raindrops in a heavy storm.

Those at the front of the crowd stopped as though they had rammed into a brick wall. An instant later, with the deadly hail of lead continuing and knowing that the slightest lift of Lucas' arm would center his sights on them, they were turning, screaming, clawing, punching at those behind as they tried to put distance between themselves and the rifle.

For perhaps a second of time the mob was a struggling mass—but only for a second. Then it seemed to fly apart as though a giant keg of powder had exploded somewhere in its midst, hurtling men off down the street like leaves being blown by a hard wind.

It had ceased to be a mob, had become a hundred or so badly scared men, each of them intent on putting as much distance as possible, as fast as possible, between himself and Lucas McCain.

Mark had a last glimpse of Smithers, who went in a head-long dive over the side of the wagon, then scrambled away on his hands and knees along the walk.

He saw Lucas stand a minute, looking grimly after those running from him. Then his father turned, bent to Micah, and gave him a hand up. With the marshal leaning against Lucas, the two crossed the walk again and went into Micah's office, closing the door behind them.

Mark discovered his lungs were aching. He had been holding his breath during those moments when Lucas had broken and scattered that mob. Now he breathed deeply, still watching.

Not all of the men were still running. A few had stopped and were gathering in little groups, off at a prudent distance, for some loud, angry talk, glaring toward Micah's office. But they didn't seem inclined to start moving in that direction again.

Mark turned and went at a trot up the street, with the thought that he must take the news to Dr. Harvey of what had happened to Micah and that riding Latigo might make him too conspicuous now, at a time when the name of McCain was not at all popular in North Fork.

Nearing the Madera House, he saw the young doctor come out from the lobby and get into his buggy, probably just leaving the bedside of Rufus Dabney. Mark called to him and ran into the street. Dr. Harvey pulled up.

"Only Micah hurt?" he commented, as Mark hurriedly told him what had happened. "I heard the gunfire, and thought that I'd have at least a dozen patients to patch up. All right, I'll hurry on down there. And you had better get off the street until tempers cool down, Mark."

This was good advice. Mark had already thought of the advisability of it, himself, but with some question as to

where he should go. It was getting pretty late now, probably close on to midnight, and he didn't want to bother
anybody by waking them up at such an hour.

He could sit and wait in the hotel lobby, of course, but
that would be a pretty lonely business, with no telling
when Lucas would be ready to ride back to the ranch. And
Mark just didn't want to sit around if he could make
himself useful.

While turning this over in his head, he started walking
east along Prairie Street. The town seemed pretty quiet
now. He would make his way to Lucas, Mark told himself, and let his father decide what he should do. Also, he
wanted to find out how Micah was.

Mark turned into an alley which ran back of the buildings
on the east side of Main Street. The place which served
Micah as office and jail had two entrances, and the rear one
was on this alley.

He trudged hurriedly along over the alley ruts—and
walked headlong into disaster.

It was very dark—nobody bothered with burning expen-
sive coal oil to keep night lamps lighted on the alley—and
the only warning he had was the scrape of a footstep, the
shift of a black shadow from a doorway, somebody moving

quickly toward him and reaching out.

Mark tried to run. He managed to take only one step when a hand clamped over his mouth and jerked him up short. A voice muttered, "Stand still, boy. Keep quiet and you won't be hurt."

He would have known that voice anywhere. It belonged to Travis Benteen! And it seemed as though he knew ahead of time—as another black shadow approached him, with the brief flare of a match cupped in a pair of hands for a look at his face, then quickly blown out—who else was here.

Sid Cade chuckled, a harsh, menacing sort of sound. "McCain's kid!" he exclaimed.

An icy feather seemed to brush along Mark's spine. He stood rigid, Benteen's hand still over his mouth.

"The one who was lippy with me," Cade went on. "And I haven't forgotten that!"

"Shut up, Cade," Benteen growled. "He's not to be hurt, and if you forget that for a single second, you'll be answering to me."

"Sure!" Cade muttered angrily. "Just turn him loose, after apologizing because we bumped into him, and let this sprat go spread the news that we're here!"

"Don't you ever use your head?" Benteen said impatiently. "We came to this town for only one reason—to break Jeter out of the cell where they've shoved him. And we can use the boy. He'll get us through the door yonder without any need to shoot our way in."

"Yeah? Well, I'd prefer to go in shooting—with every bullet in my gun notched for McCain himself!"

"It's going to be played just the way I've lined it out!" Benteen snapped. Then he pushed Mark forward. "Start walking—slow and easy."

Mark obeyed him. He had no other choice.

They reached the rear door at Micah's place, which was flush with the alley. Benteen took his hand away from Mark's mouth. "Knock, now. Whoever answers, name yourself and say you've got something to tell your father. No more than that. Heed me, boy!"

Both men were crowding close to him. Mark banged his knuckles against the door. It was Micah's night deputy who answered him, "Who's there?"

He said, "It's me, Mark McCain. I want to tell my father something."

A mutter of voices came from the other side of the door. Then a lock clicked and it swung open. Lucas himself was

standing there, with lamplight behind him.

Benteen shoved Mark hard and he stumbled over a low sill, almost falling as he entered what was the back room. With a harsh rasp in his voice, Benteen commanded, "Reach, everybody! Lucas, get them high and hold them there!"

Lucas put out a hand to steady Mark, then obeyed the order, both arms lifting. His face was tight.

The night deputy was standing with hands high also. Across the room Micah was sitting laxly in an armchair, both shirt and undershirt off, Dr. Harvey working on his arm.

Dr. Harvey looked around with no change of expression. "I never carry a gun," he said. "And this man needs my care. I intend to give it to him."

The gun gripped in Travis Benteen's fist seemed to waver for a moment, indecisively. Then he nodded. "Sure, Doc. You go right ahead. No telling when I might have to call on you for some patching up, myself!"

The town jail consisted of four cells, with iron-barred doors and windows, two on each side of the room. The man Lucas had captured and brought in stood in the only cell which was occupied, impatiently rattling the door. "You took long enough showing up, Benteen! There was a crowd outside only a couple of minutes ago, yelling about stringing me up. Get me out of here!"

Lucas had backed off several steps, with a slight jerk of his head which told Mark to stand clear of him. Mark moved to one side, stopping when he reached a corner. Dr. Harvey was working as though nobody else were there. He murmured, "You're lucky, Micah, no bones broken. But you won't be using this arm for a while."

Sid Cade was watching Lucas, with an expression of overbearing hatred on his face. He was remembering how he had hit the dirt from fear of Lucas' rifle. Then he was looking around the room, and realizing he was searching for the deadly long-gun, Mark looked also. He didn't see it anywhere.

Lucas' attention was fixed on Cade, who, like Benteen, had a pistol gripped in his fist. But when Lucas spoke, it was not to Cade. "Trav," he said, "you're getting in deeper with every move you make."

Benteen smiled. "You going to warn me, Lucas, that I'm liable to draw a black mark if I break Jeter out of here—that I'll have a posse coming after me?" Then he laughed. "A posse made up those who ran when you popped a few bullets at their feet—who hadn't the sense to realize you'd never raise your sights against them?"

Benteen laughed again. "I like it around here. Plenty of chances for rich pickings—think I'll stay awhile. And you're the one who'll draw the black mark, Lucas, for driving that mob off, saving Jeter for me. Maybe it'll bring you over to my side yet."

Lucas' features seemed to grow tighter still. Micah, who had been sitting with his head down on his chest, looked up to study Lucas thoughtfully.

Cade said bitingly, "Benteen, every time you and McCain get together, it's nothing but gab! How about shaking Jeter out?"

"Yes," Benteen agreed and pointed his gun at Micah. "You—Marshal—where are the keys to that cell? And don't try any stalling!"

"Don't intend to, with those guns on us," Micah answered quietly. "My deputy there has the keys."

Cade went instantly to the deputy, ramming his gun into the man's stomach. "Get that door open!"

The deputy stumbled toward the cell door, fumbling the keys out of his pocket. But his hands were shaking so hard he couldn't fit the right one in the lock. Cade gave him a

furious shove which sent the man staggering aside. He fell
to the floor and stayed there.

Sid Cade opened the door. Jeter came rushing out. Benteen jerked his head commandingly at the man and both
of them started backing toward the alley. But Cade did
not follow them. His attention, hard and vengeful, was on
Lucas again.

"I've got some unfinished business here," he informed
Benteen, "with this long-legged rifle-packer!"

"No," Benteen said. "We're finished here and pulling
out."

Cade turned on him savagely. "I get rid of people who
bother me—and this jasper has come at us twice already,
made us run!"

"He won't be doing it again," Benteen said. "Come on,
Cade."

But the outlaw hesitated, mouth working angrily. His
gun was now pointed almost at Benteen, and Benteen's
was pointed almost at him. For a breathless second Mark
thought perhaps everything would be settled right here.

Then Benteen, without taking his gaze from Cade, used
his left hand to lift another gun from his belt. He tossed
this to Jeter, who caught the weapon deftly and turned its

muzzle in Cade's direction. He was backing up his boss.

With both of them against him, Cade jammed his own gun furiously back in its holster. "All right! He gets off, this time. But at least I'm taking his rifle along, so it won't be used against us again! It must be somewhere here—"

"Where's the sense in that?" Benteen demanded. "He'd be only a shade less sharp, using any rifle, and he could grab up a Winchester right in this office if he meant to come after us. But he won't. And we're wasting time, Cade; let's get going."

Cade gnawed his lip for a moment, then nodded in surly fashion and started moving. All of them backed toward the door. Cade, the last one out, sent a final look at Lucas McCain. "Next time," he said, "it'll be a lot different!"

Then he slammed the door, from outside, with a crash which shook the whole building.

After that, there was a long moment of silence. The night deputy pulled himself up shamefacedly from the floor and went into the front part of the building.

Dr. Harvey said, as matter-of-factly as though nothing at all had happened, "Have to find something, now, to rig a sling for your arm, Micah."

"Whatever's necessary," the marshal said, a little testily. "Just get finished with me!"

Micah looked to the alley door, from that to his hurt arm which he held stiffly, and shook his head. "Can't go after them myself," he muttered.

He glanced then after his night deputy and shook his head again, indicating that a man who had shown such fear couldn't handle the job either.

Lucas stirred. "If you'd like me to try for their trail, Micah—"

"No," Micah said wearily. "I'd like plenty to ask it of you, Lucas—would like asking you to put on my badge and take my job until I'm fit again. But I can't. Not after all that's happened."

Lucas nodded. It was evident he had expected this reply.

"Not much use trying to do anything now, anyway," Micah continued. "Too dark out, no moon. Come morning, I'll pick about a dozen men, swear them in as a posse, and start hunting for that bunch—"

Dr. Harvey interrupted him. "You're not going to do any riding tomorrow, Micah!"

The marshal snorted. "Just put this arm in a sling, Doc. I'll ride!"

He rubbed his face then. "Some of those I'll have to swear in—because there are so few good ones around who'll be willing to ride posse—were in the mob tonight."

"And most of them pretty ashamed by now that they were," Lucas said. "Also, I doubt that any townsman fired the bullet that hit you—more likely, it was some drifter."

He turned suddenly and went into the front room. Mark moved to a bench nearby and sat down. His knees felt shaky.

And he was overwhelmed by a sense of having behaved badly, of having done the wrong thing. Mark was thinking that it was because of him Trav Benteen and Sid Cade had had such an easy time of it, taking the prisoner out of his cell.

Lucas came back. He had his rifle now, balanced in both hands, and murmured, "A man has a lesson pounded into him—then, a moment comes along, and for no reason at all he forgets—"

"Huh?" Micah said.

"I underestimated Benteen, just didn't think he would risk coming in here after Jeter," Lucas explained. "Also, I shot my rifle empty, breaking up that mob, and laid it aside in your office without reloading."

"As I remember, you had a pretty good reason, your hands full, helping me," Micah said.

Lucas smiled wryly. "Yes. And at that, maybe a good thing, this one time, that I did forget."

"A mighty good thing!" Micah agreed fervently. "If you'd had that rifle in your hands, loaded, when those two busted in here—"

He didn't have to finish. Things could have been a lot different. Mark shivered a little, inwardly, visualizing what might have happened. Micah was counting the loss of Jeter as something which was less important than the possibility that bullets might have been flying wildly in this room.

Lucas said, then, "Mark and I can stick around a while longer, if you think it's necessary—"

"No. Thanks for the offer, but you and the boy can go home," Micah said. "And that isn't all. . . ." He hesitated.

Lucas said, "Go on."

"Stay there—please!" Micah said. "Leave Benteen and that Cade to me. Maybe I can't handle them, maybe nobody can, but don't you try it again, Lucas. One more thing that ties you in any way to them—"

"I know," Lucas said quietly.

"Let it be said, anyway. Another mob might be on the move, one nobody can stop—heading straight for your ranch!" Micah said.

And maybe it would happen anyway, Mark thought.

Still—with his chin stiffening—he would be there, with Lucas. They would face whatever might come, together.

9   Under Suspicion

The McCains rode home through the thick darkness, letting their tired mounts have their own heads, set their own pace.

It was very late, the latest Mark had ever been up; but tomorrow was Sunday, when they usually slept a little longer anyway.

For about half the distance back along the road, Lucas did not say a word. He was, Mark knew, turning over in his head everything that had happened today, trying to form some plans for the future—and probably being severe with himself about what he figured were the mistakes he had made.

Mark didn't think his father had made any mistakes, even in putting his rifle aside with all its loads spent. After a while he ventured to say this aloud, adding that it looked

like he was the one who had made a wrong move, heading
for Micah's office by way of that alley door.

"I'm not going to chide you any for doing that," Lucas
said. "Would much rather not have had you involved,
of course, but Benteen and Cade would have found a way
in other than the one they used, if you hadn't come along
—probably one that would have been a lot rougher on
everybody."

This was true, Mark realized, recalling what Benteen
had said about them shooting their way in, if necessary. Not
that he should take any credit for preventing that. He had
simply happened to be handy for Benteen to use.

"I can't understand why that crowd of people didn't
think about the alley door," Mark said. "They could have
beaten it down and taken Jeter out that way."

"Yes. They could have," Lucas agreed. "Micah and I
couldn't have guarded both doors. But a mob doesn't think.
It is like a blind, senseless animal which does things that
have no rhyme or reason. It turns men into savages—such
as Smithers, for instance, that saddle maker who made the
speech, ordinarily as mild-mannered a fellow as anyone
would want to know."

Mark said, "You and Micah didn't seem to be worried

that those people in the street might get together again and cause more trouble."

"We weren't," Lucas said, suddenly yawning. "Once a mob can be turned and started running, it isn't at all likely to come together again for more mischief. The men in it feel shame because they are running, and then further shame at having let themselves become involved in such a business in the first place. There'll be no more trouble in North Fork tonight."

But there could be more trouble later, aimed at the McCains, if Trav Benteen and his bunch struck again.

They made the familiar approach to their own place. Everything seemed in order there, the house and barn dark, very still. But Lucas made Mark halt at a little distance and wait while he went ahead on foot to check, moving alertly, seeming to disappear immediately, making no more noise than a prowling Comanche.

It was some time before he came back, appearing again with a low hail: "All quiet, Mark. Barn lantern's lighted. Let's unsaddle."

Mark was suddenly very tired, and his eyes felt as though they were trying to glue themselves together. But there were certain things to be done, and done right, before he satisfied his desire for sleep: Latigo's saddle to be removed and pegged, his blanket to be shaken out and spread carefully to dry, and then the pony to be rubbed down and checked before being turned into the corral.

Latigo, of course, would roll in the bed of sand provided in a corner of the corral. Still, as Lucas had put it forcefully: "A man who doesn't think first of his horse, every time and all the time, is sure to find himself afoot some day when he needs a horse bad. Don't let that happen to you, Mark!"

He splashed some cold water on his face and felt better, then tackled the unsaddling. And he said, "Pa, you meant to capture Trav Benteen and Cade today, didn't you—if you could?"

"Yes," Lucas admitted, and stood for a moment with his jaw hard and mouth tight, reviewing all that had happened in that quest for the outlaws.

"And then turn them over to Micah?"

Lucas only nodded this time, resuming his own unsaddling. "It's what I meant when I said I hoped to end the worries of your Aunt Susan and cousin Madge about Trav, while heaping another kind of grief on their heads, for which they would probably hate me. If Benteen keeps on, he's going to end up in a way that'll break their hearts; whereas if he served out the sentence that the law says is needful to pay for what he has done, it would be hard on them for a while, but there would be the chance that, once it was finished, he'd try a different kind of life, one they could share with him."

Lucas hung his big saddle on its peg and yawned again. He was tired too. "As for Cade, he will probably be in prison the rest of his life, if caught—and justly so. The other three in that bunch need taking, also, but they aren't nearly as important."

"Benteen didn't seem to be worried that you'd come after him again," Mark observed.

"He was giving me a warning that he doesn't intend to let me even get close to him again," Lucas said. "That is, with my sights fined down in a try to take him—"

Mark's father caught himself, then, and closed the subject, hazing Razor toward the corral. Mark looked around, decided everything was in order, and started toward the house. But Lucas, coming along after him, cleared his throat and said, "Mark, a nice warm night, how about us sleeping outdoors for a change?"

Mark was slightly startled. They hadn't done any sleeping in the open since the house was finished.

"I've already brought our blankets out. Suppose we spread them among those cottonwoods over beyond the springhouse. . . " Lucas suggested.

The reason for it was plain enough. If anybody came along in the night, planning to make trouble, they wouldn't be caught inside—but would be out in the open, in a good position to fight back.

They slept out every night from then on, for a while, leaving the house after supper and not returning to it until sunup.

Mark liked it a lot. They would lie stretched out under the stars, tired but feeling good, and Lucas would talk, stories of trail herds crossing Red River; of his days in the Nations, the outlaw territory; of fighting Comanches in the wild *llano*.

A number of days passed. There was, as usual, plenty to keep them busy through every minute of daylight. The garden was growing by leaps and bounds, with constant hoe work required by Mark. The chickens had to be tended, though they seemed to gobble a lot of grain to no purpose, with nothing showing in the nests which Mark had hopefully arranged for eggs. He was beginning to watch those nests with some anxiety.

Lucas began building a couple of rooms in the barn. One was a sort of tack room, for the storage of all their leather gear. The other was planned for the day when they would acquire more acreage and would need a hired hand to help work a larger ranch.

They had news, people passing by or coming out from town to visit them. Things were quiet for several days; then word came that Benteen and his bunch had struck again, another Texas cattleman packing a lot of money. Then they hit Dandy Griffin's stagecoach, north of the river, taking a mine payroll which was being shipped in the express box.

Micah led his posse in a three-day sweep to the south and west. They came back empty-handed.

Lucas was driving himself very hard. It was as though he was trying to lose himself in work in order to keep from thinking about the menace of Benteen and Cade. He rode away one morning and came back with six yearlings, bought from the proceeds of the sale of the two-year-olds. More would be along later; meanwhile, this batch would be held on the feed lot for a while, then worked gradually in with the herd. It was Mark's job to check on them constantly. He was becoming as busy as Lucas.

Then Aunt Susan and Madge came out from town again.

While Mrs. Benteen and Lucas sat on the porch and talked, as before, Mark showed Madge the yearlings. She seemed very subdued and quiet, not much interested. Mark ventured to ask whether there had been any word yet from her father.

Madge glanced at him sharply and then away, shaking her head. Mark went on, "He must know now you're in North Fork. That fellow Jeter must have told him."

"I guess so," Madge admitted. "We keep hoping for a message. But it hasn't come."

He suggested that they saddle up and take a ride; Madge was wearing a blue dress with a sash and a big bow in the back, but could borrow his gear again. She said, "No. I just don't feel like it."

Mark was dismayed to see tears on her cheeks. He realized she was weeping and reached out to take her hand, to make a try at comforting her. But she turned away, dabbing at her eyes with her finger. "I'll be all right. I'm not crying for myself. It's the way they're treating Mamma!"

Everybody in North Fork knew by now that Aunt Susan

was Trav Benteen's wife and Madge his daughter. Some were saying they should be forced to leave the Madera House, even that they should be run out of town. And their money was running low. Madge didn't know what they were going to do.

"I guess we'll have to go back to Texas—without seeing Papa at all," she said. Then she burst out, "People are awful! They stare at me as though I had horns on my head!"

She and her mother returned to North Fork presently, after refusing an invitation to stay for lunch. Lucas frowningly watched them go, then revealed he had given Mrs. Benteen some money, all he could spare.

"No amount of talk is going to make Judge Hanavan turn them out of the Madera House," he told Mark, referring to their kindly friend who owned the hotel. "The judge assured your Aunt Susan that she and Madge can stay as long as they wish, and he isn't pressing them for payment of their room rent."

"Wouldn't it be best if they returned to Texas?" Mark ventured.

"Best all around," Lucas agreed. "But they aren't going to do it, no matter what is said or done, as long as there is any chance at all of seeing Benteen."

He sighed then, shaking his head. "Trav will try to set up a meeting. And it's going to cause bad trouble when he does. Micah is still having Susan watched."

The following day they had more visitors, Dr. and Mrs. Harvey, who did stay for lunch—a lunch at which the first of the roasting ears and the first fried chicken were eaten.

Mrs. Harvey shook her head ruefully, when the meal was completed. "Lucas, a man who cooks as you do makes a woman feel completely useless!"

"You deserve the credit!" Lucas said, smiling. "Mark told me about the special way you fix fried chicken. I just followed his directions."

He and the young doctor moved outside for some talk, and Mrs. Harvey turned to Mark with a conspiratorial air, taking a small paper sack from her purse. "Here's the powdered sugar I promised you, Mark."

"Gosh, thanks," he said gratefully. "I've only got a few days left. And those doggoned chickens haven't laid any eggs yet!"

"My hens aren't laying very well either," Mrs. Harvey said. "But I'll find at least a couple of eggs for you someplace, if necessary. Don't worry about it."

When their friends drove away in the doctor's buggy, Lucas revealed that Dr. Harvey had brought disquieting news. Benteen's bunch had struck again—at the Big T ranch, fifty miles west of town. Jeff Trent, who owned the place, had been forced to open his safe, then had been pistol-whipped. The proceeds of a sale he had just made, reported to be at least five thousand dollars, had been taken.

"Trav is covering a lot of territory, hitting in widely separated places," Lucas said. "It makes Micah's job of trying to catch him an awfully difficult one."

The next day there was still another visitor—Rufus Dabney, sitting in the back of a rented surrey, bandages showing under his hat. One of the Gem Livery's hostlers was handling the reins.

He leaned out to grip Lucas' hand and squeezed it strongly. "I'm heading on north, had to come and tell that I've never believed for a minute you tipped Trav Benteen I was packing the pay cash for my trail crew," he said.

"You should know, Rufe, that I never believed for a minute you'd hold such a thought," Lucas replied.

"A mean, cold-eyed fellow gave me a couple of licks

with his Colt barrel after Trav stopped me and they found the money," Dabney continued. "Guess they were pretty sure I had it—Trav knows my habits, from the past."

"The mean, cold-eyed fellow wears the name of Cade," Lucas told him.

"Micah Torrance told me the same thing. Then, when my boys found and picked me up, I did some babbling, out of my head, mentioned I had run into you, and they jumped fast to a wrong conclusion: that you passed word to Trav about the money, then brought Micah one of Trav's bunch, meaning to help him get loose again to cover yourself. I rawhided them all pretty good, just as soon as I was up and around."

"We both know the way it all really happened," Lucas said. "Let's let it go at that, Rufe."

"Sure," the big Texan agreed, and held out his hand again. "Well, Lucas, so long until next summer, when I'll be seeing you and Mark once more."

"I hope so," Lucas said slowly. "I hope you'll find us right here."

Rufus Dabney studied him and grimly nodded in complete understanding. "What Trav Benteen is doing makes things pretty rough for you, all right. But hang on!"

"I mean to," Lucas said. Then, as Rufus Dabney settled back and was driven away again, he added, apparently forgetting that Mark was listening, "But sometimes meaning to isn't enough, when you're only one man against a crowd. . . ."

They worked the herd that afternoon, moving it to fresh graze in the south pasture, and then checked the fence. Mark enjoyed this, as he did everything which involved saddle work. Of course, as Lucas had often pointed out, a cattleman had so many different jobs to handle that he was more often out of saddle than in it.

They found a couple of minor breaks and some sagging strands. "I think we'll ride to town after supper and pick up a reel of wire so we can make some repairs," Lucas said. "That okay with you, son?"

Mark had a moment of thinking it strange they should leave the ranch, where things were quiet, only to pick up some wire in town, where they might not be. . . . This was an errand which could just as well wait for a Saturday shopping trip, but he had a hunch there was another reason for Lucas' proposal and loyally said, "Sure!"

So they set out in the cool of the evening, and—maybe

because Lucas planned it that way—arrived on Main Street just when it was nearly full dark.

This was the supper hour in North Fork, few people on the walks, most of the stores just closing. But Lucas didn't seem in any hurry to pick up the wire. Instead, they stopped at the North Fork General Store, where Lucas had a brief talk with Hattie Denton, its owner.

Then they headed out again and south along the walk, Lucas shortening his long-legged stride so Mark could keep up. Passing Micah's office, Mark glanced through a barred window and saw a strange man, raw-boned and hard-faced, sitting within. "New night deputy, named Pete Nader," Lucas remarked. "Micah fired the other one."

The fellow who had shown fear when Jeter was broken free, Mark remembered.

They paused at Nils Swenson's blacksmith shop, and Lucas had a brief word with big-muscled Nils, who was hammering on a cherry-red circle of iron which would be fitted as a tire on a freighter's wagon. Mark heard Nils say, "You need help, Lucas, yoost call. I'll come runnin'—and not alone!"

Banker Hamilton was next, and after him Judge Hanavan, who was standing on the porch at the Madera

House. Mark heard the judge say, "Don't worry, Lucas, Mrs. Benteen and her daughter can stay as long as they like; they can't be blamed for what Trav is doing. And those of us who know you are certain that you can't be either."

They started back. Lucas murmured, "A man never realizes just how valuable good friends can be, until a time like this comes along—"

Then he stopped short, halting Mark also, with a hand on his arm.

A number of men were clustered on the walk ahead, maybe six or eight, blocking the walk. Mark didn't know any of them.

One said, "There they are—McCain and that kid of his! Bold as brass!"

"Hey, McCain!" another yelled. "When are you going to bring in another of Benteen's bunch, make another big play to cover yourself, with the scut free almost before Micah can turn the key on him?"

Harsh, goading laughter greeted that thrust. Lucas was standing silently—the rifle in his hand; he made no move to lift it.

One of those men suddenly turned aside, grabbed up

something and threw it. Mark ducked instinctively, though the missile didn't seem to come close. It chunked against wood, probably a rock.

Another bent to look for something to throw, but froze as Lucas spoke.

"Come on, Mark," he said, and started moving forward, straight at them.

Mark's legs felt curiously wooden as he moved too, in obedience to Lucas' order. Side by side they walked together, Lucas still showing no sign he meant to use his rifle.

The men waited in taut silence, blocking the walk.

"Get out of the way," Lucas told them quietly. "We're coming through."

No sound came from them, no move. It didn't look as though they were going to do it.

10   Night Raid!

But a way opened up for Lucas and Mark McCain, the men stepping aside. Maybe it was the quiet force in Lucas' voice which persuaded them to move back, or maybe it was the menace of the rifle, carried easily and unobtrusively in his hand.

And maybe, too, Mark thought, it was the pride in Lucas, which refused to let him retreat from such riffraff, which made him walk tall, not turning his head by as much as a fraction of an inch even to look at them or to recognize the fact they were there, as he passed by.

Mark stretched himself to walk tall, also, to behave exactly as his father was behaving. Their heels pounded the planks of the walk together. Lucas gestured for Mark to mount first, then swung himself into saddle on Razor, a move so swift and sure there wasn't a second when the rifle wasn't ready for instant use.

Micah Torrance's new deputy, Pete Nader, suddenly was there, coming with a rush from across the street. He snapped, "What's going on here? You trying to start trouble, McCain?"

"No," Lucas answered coldly.

The deputy looked toward the men on the walk, now clustered together again. "Looks like it to me!"

"If you want to believe that, go ahead," Lucas told him, even more coldly.

Nader stared up at him. "Micah's out with the posse. He left word about you—that you're under orders to stay on your ranch."

"It wasn't an order, but an agreement between Micah and me," Lucas said. "I agreed to stay there for a while, but didn't say anything about making that stay indefinite. Now, get out of the way. My son and I are going home."

Nader did not move. "I could hold you here until he gets back," the deputy said threateningly.

"You could try," Lucas conceded. "But I doubt that you will."

Mark realized there was a contest of wills between the two men, the deputy probably trying to find out how far

Lucas might be pushed. He must have decided it wasn't very far, since he stepped aside and muttered, "All right. Get back to your place. And this time—stay there!"

Lucas did not bother to answer. He gigged Razor. Mark urged Latigo alongside his father's black. They started up the street.

For the first time, Mark noticed people scattered unobtrusively here and there: Judge Hanavan, with what looked like a shotgun under his arm; Nils Swenson, swinging in one hand his big single-jack hammer, which Mark couldn't lift with both hands; Banker Hamilton, strolling quietly along the walk, lifting his hand in silent salutation as they passed by.

Others, too—all, Mark realized, ready to lend a hand in case any trouble had developed.

Presently he ventured a comment. "That's a tough deputy who's working for Micah now."

"Too tough," Lucas said. "Too ready, for some reason, to get in a tangle with me. I think Micah must have hired him in a hurry, without a chance to make a close check on the man. From what I've seen and heard there's a feeling in me Nader is playing some game of his own. I wish I knew what it is he's up to . . . ."

Which only made things even more complicated, Mark thought as they stopped at the hardware store for the wire, if Micah had a deputy who was working against him. And Mark wondered again just what the real reason had been for this trip he and Lucas had made to North Fork tonight.

No explanation was forthcoming until they were spreading their blankets under the trees by the springhouse and Lucas said, "Mark, did you recognize any of those men in that bunch on the walk?"

He shook his head. "They looked just like a bunch of drifters to me, Pa."

Such people were constantly to be seen in North Fork, part of the great, restless movement which was settling the vast emptiness of the West. Some were honest, purposeful men, looking for the right place to settle, the right chance to grow big in the years ahead.

But others were of a different breed, the kind who would probably always remain drifters, of no particular good to themselves or anybody else.

"That's what I decided too," Lucas said. "Loafers, ready to make trouble for us because they hadn't anything to lose and maybe something to gain. There were some of them in that mob the other night also. Whenever there's any senseless mischief being planned, you'll find them on hand."

"I heard what they yelled about your letting Jeter escape, about planning it to happen that way," Mark said. "How could they believe such a thing?"

"Son, you'll discover some people always find it easy to believe certain things, because that happens to fit in with what they want to do," Lucas said.

He was going through his nightly ritual of checking the rifle and continued, "I made that ride tonight because I had to find out at first hand what the people in North Fork are saying and thinking about us."

Lucas unloaded the magazine and tested the ejector's spring tension. "I could have dropped you off to visit the Harveys, Mark, but am glad now that I didn't—that you saw and heard what happened. Just facing the easy things isn't going to equip you to make out in what at times is a pretty tough world."

He began to reload again. "Well, we both found out. Those who count with us—our friends—aren't believing for a minute that we're in any way helping Trav Benteen and his bunch."

Far off, north of the river, a hunting wolf bayed in the night. The cartridges made a dull snicking sound against metal as Lucas filled the magazine.

"Whether that helps us very much or not, I don't know," Lucas went on. "Unfortunately, there are a lot of the other kind of people around, who do believe we're helping Benteen, sharing in his stolen loot—or who want to believe it because that suits certain purposes they have in mind."

"Let them!" Mark said indignantly. "We'll be ready if they want to try anything!"

"I hope so," Lucas said. "I was advised not to risk a tangle with the drifters—could have backed away from that bunch and there'd have been plenty of help if they had tried to come at us—"

He paused, as though mentally reviewing what he had done, and then continued, "But backing away from anything is a bad habit to get into. The best way to handle trouble is always to meet it head on. Besides, I was thinking about something else which might happen later, and decided to make a move that I hoped would force it to happen . . . ."

Lucas stood up. Mark said, throat a little dry and tight, "What might happen, Pa? When?"

Lucas was a tall silhouette against a dark sky. His head turned, toward some sound which seemed to come from the direction of the river. "Get under your blankets, Mark. I'll make a quick check and join you in a few minutes."

He returned some minutes later. Mark, half-asleep, realized Lucas was settling down beside him. Latigo nickered drowsily in the corral. Then it was very quiet.

Mark dozed. He awakened with a start—and sat up to discover Lucas was gone.

There was faint light from the setting moon, low in the sky. It showed Lucas, soundlessly crossing the yard from the barn toward the silent house. He stayed there for several minutes, then headed toward the corral. Razor snorted inquiringly. Mark heard his father speak soothingly to the horse.

He came in the direction of the springhouse, then. Mark huddled down in his blankets. Lucas was already worried enough; he didn't want to add to those worries, though he ached to join in the night vigil, the watch over everything Lucas was obviously keeping.

Mark breathed hard, regularly, deeply, pretending that he was asleep. Lucas came in among the trees and stopped. He stood for some time there. Mark did not know when he went away, because it was done so silently, but all at once Lucas was no longer near him.

And all at once, too, the pleasure of sleeping out-of-doors, under the stars, was gone for Mark.

He longed desperately for the safety and security of his own bunk under the tight roof of the house yonder. He remembered how good that bunk felt on nights when violent prairie thunderstorms raged, with blinding flashes of lightning, thunder so loud it seemed the very heavens were splitting open. And how warm and snug it was on winter nights, too, when the icy wind howled out of the north and rattled the shutters.

Along with those remembrances, there were others of nights when he just settled wearily down for a long, deep sleep until Lucas' hand squeezed his shoulder, with a cheery "Daylight's wasting, son. Up and out!"

Mark wanted it to be that way again. But—with a tickle of fear—maybe it never would be. Maybe all that was happening would grow to some act of violence which would destroy the peace and security he and Lucas had known here.

He rolled out of his blankets, stood up and went to the edge of the trees.

Nothing was to be seen from there, though—nothing at all. No sign of Lucas, no stir of movement to identify where he might be—only the house and barn, the corral, the familiar things which somehow looked so different at night. And the only sound came from the faint gurgle of water in the irrigation ditch.

Mark stayed where he was for some time, with temptation clawing at him to leave the shelter of these trees and to go hunting for Lucas. But he knew this wouldn't do, that he was in as safe a place as there was for him. It became one of the hardest things he had ever done, though, just to stay put, while time passed and the stars wheeled slowly overhead.

Lucas knew how to tell time by the stars. It was something Mark hadn't yet learned. There was a very late feel in the air, however, probably well past midnight—and still no sign of Lucas.

Then, suddenly, Mark realized he and his father were no longer alone here, that they had company, but of a sort who meant them no good!

A stir of horses, first, on the road from town, riders approaching so cautiously that Mark wasn't aware of them until they were only about a quarter of a mile away. Maybe the same ones who had faced Lucas and himself on the walk in North Fork—it seemed likely, at least—with sense enough not to make any unnecessary noise which would warn of their coming.

They stopped to confer together, voices so low as not to be audible, while Mark continued to scan the yard for Lucas. But there was still no sight or sound to indicate where he might be.

The riders came on, fanning out as they passed the corral and approached the yard, still moving cautiously. They were probably thinking of Lucas' deadly rifle.

Mark tried to make a count of them and couldn't; they were just dim shapes yonder, muttering together again. There were at least five of them, though, he thought, and, in all likelihood, even more.

Then one of them laughed and spoke out: "We're behaving like a bunch of spooked old women! Nothing here to be scared of! He must be in the house, along with the kid. I say hit it, spray plenty of lead, put some bullets around their ears, then use some more to keep them running when they come busting out!"

There was a general babble of excited agreement. The same man continued, "Spread out a little more now. We'll

make a pass at the house, riding fast, then swing around and come back—"

Lucas McCain's voice cut in on him, cold and biting, "You, big mouth! I've got you right in my sights. Turn around and clear out of here, with no more talk, or you get the first bullet!"

Lucas was nowhere near either the house or the barn. Instead, he was almost directly opposite where Mark stood, somewhere at the edge of the grass where the south pasture began, probably stretched out flat there.

For a moment after he spoke, those horsemen all seemed frozen where they were, caught completely by surprise. Then one of them yelled recklessly and pulled trigger.

Lucas' rifle whiplashed instantly in response, and in the next minute so many things happened that nobody could possibly have kept track of them all.

Men shouted, firing wildly in the darkness, driving their mounts this way and that in the yard. Mark heard bullets rattle like hail against the siding of the house. He saw one of the horsemen coming toward him and leaped to hug one of the trees, while more bullets whistled among the leaves overhead. But the man turned his horse and went plunging back again.

Lucas was using his rifle steadily, spacing the shots with deliberation, its sharp snapping sound cutting through the deeper barking of the handguns with which the intruders all seemed armed. Mark heard one of them cry out and saw him fall from saddle, then lift himself and stagger away, dragging one leg.

A moment later another one yelled, "I'm hit!" He pitched forward, wrapped both arms around his horse's neck and spurred it away at a run.

Lucas called, "The rest of you—get going while you're still able!" and Mark realized his father had shifted position and was now firing across the yard, using the rifle to herd them back toward town.

The horses of those who still remained milled about for a second. Mark heard a snatch of angry argument, some man shouting, "He's all alone—we can run him down!"

The rifle lashed again. Another man yelled, "You try it, if you're a mind to—I'm getting out of here!"

He took off, racing toward the road. Others followed him, moving at equal speed, until only two men were left in the yard. One of those emptied his gun in a final burst of wild firing, hammering the bullets to all corners of the yard. Lucas waited until he was finished, then pulled trigger a last time. Those two broke and ran also.

The whole bunch stopped, off at some distance, for some threatening yells. They did not come back, but instead trailed on toward town.

A horse had been left behind, moving about in an erratic circle, nickering fearfully. Lucas spoke quietly: "Mark—"

"Yes, Pa?" Mark answered while leaving the sheltering safety of the trees and moving out in front of the spring-house.

"There's a man over by the corral. I'll go see about him. You come and pick up this horse," Lucas told him.

The horse had stepped on its own reins, had become entangled in them. Mark straightened out the lines, with soothing talk. The horse quieted down. Mark held him, waiting on Lucas.

His father, who had worked to and through the barn, came out in the corral and moved across it toward the pole fence. A whisper of voices came from there. Then Lucas called, "Bring him here, Mark."

Lucas was outside the fence now, standing over a man, the one Mark had seen fall from his saddle, then drag himself away. He was down on his side, moaning in pain. "My leg!" he whimpered.

"You got off easy," Lucas told him coldly. "Night-riding, throwing your bullets around, risking the hurt of a boy .... You're plenty lucky it was only your leg that happened to get hit."

"Those others'll be back! And more with them!" the man threatened.

"You spread the word: anybody who tries such a thing again will get the same welcome. Now quit your whining and use your good leg to stand on. I want you gone from here."

Lucas lent a hand and the fellow managed to make it to his saddle. He rode slowly away.

Looking after him, Mark said, "Pa—you didn't aim to miss—like before—did you?"

"No," Lucas replied. "When everything a man values most is being threatened, he doesn't aim to miss."

"Do you think they'll be back—tonight?"

"I doubt it. But we'd better not count on there not being another try."

Lucas looked after the retreating man then also. "Doc Harvey won't thank me for having to climb out of bed and take care of those I tagged. . . . Back to your blankets, Mark. It's late."

They walked together toward the springhouse. Lucas sent a look at the stars. "A bit past three. I'm thinking both of us are likely to be a little sleepy, come sunup."

"I'll watch," Mark offered, "and you turn in."

"Thanks," Lucas said. "But I've had experience in staying awake two days and nights on end, to keep a spooky herd from stampeding, and you haven't. Turn in, son."

Mark didn't think he could sleep again. But he did. His last recollection was of Lucas silhouetted against the stars, keeping night watch once more, the rifle ready.

11   Meeting by the River

The next thing Mark knew, Lucas was shaking him and it was gray in the east. So nothing more had happened.

Growing daylight revealed a peppering of bullet holes in the house siding. Lucas studied them somberly. "We could get some putty and close them up, Mark, but maybe it would be better just to let them stay there awhile—a reminder that nothing is won or held easy in this life."

Lucas was a little red-eyed, but tackled the day's work with his usual thoroughness. Mark felt somewhat tired himself as a result of the sleep he had lost. He was determined not to let up because of that, though.

At a little past noon a couple of horsemen appeared, surprise visitors who weren't usually seen this far from town —Judge Hanavan and Banker Hamilton. The latter's full name was John Masefield Hamilton, a portly man who talked with a Scotch burr in his voice.

Lucas went to meet them. They dismounted and walked to the shade at the springhouse, where the three talked for some time. Then the visitors came for a look at the bullet holes in the house siding. They spoke pleasant hellos to Mark, mounted up, and rode away again.

It was evident from Lucas' expression that they had not brought very good news. "Word's out in town about what happened here last night," he told Mark. "Those who tried to make trouble for us are claiming I bushwhacked them with my rifle, gave them no warning."

Mark exclaimed indignantly at this.

Lucas looked thoughtful. "There were seven of them in that bunch. I'm hoping such talk isn't being swallowed."

He revealed then that the townsmen had offered to keep watch and round up others to come and help if another move was made from North Fork against the McCains.

"I thanked them, but advised against it," Lucas said. "Judge Hanavan and Mr. Hamilton have too much at stake in town to become involved in our troubles. Besides, if there is another try, I don't think it will be made from town."

Lucas meant the marauders would probably strike from

some other direction. And there would be more men involved, Mark thought. They would have learned that seven
weren't enough to get past Lucas' rifle.

Then Lucas told the other news that the visitors had
brought. Travis Benteen's bunch had made another strike
—against a stagecoach again.

"It was carrying specie—gold-backed currency—in its
express box for a bank in Dakota Territory," Lucas revealed. "The story has it that the total was about twenty-
five thousand dollars. An express guard was shot. He isn't
in very good shape."

So Benteen's bunch was continuing its evil ways un-
checked. And, as a result, talk was now beginning against
Micah Torrance.

"Some are saying Micah isn't tough or smart enough
ever to catch Benteen," Lucas revealed. "If he doesn't do
something quick, Micah may lose his job."

Mark tried to think of North Fork without Micah wearing the marshal's badge there and couldn't. "Nobody could
do any better!" he protested.

"Probably not," Lucas agreed. "But the town is scared
that maybe it will not only lose the Texas trail-herd business, but that the stage lines will also route their coaches

away from North Fork. That would be bad."

He looked off toward the south as he spoke. Some dust showed in the sky there, indicating another herd had arrived. But there wasn't as much dust as usual at this time of year. It seemed obvious some herds were being held back, or would be headed across the river at another point, to avoid North Fork entirely.

Mark remembered how it had been last summer, how he and Lucas had visited the camps when the herds arrived, for exciting talk and stories of the trail. Maybe the opportunity wouldn't ever come again to do that.

"When people are scared, they're liable to do anything," Lucas concluded. "I'm afraid Micah will be out of a job if he doesn't make some move soon to take Benteen. And Cade, also—he's the one who shot the express guard."

It could go hard with the McCains if another man held Micah's job, one who was not particularly friendly toward them.

Lucas rode presently to check on the cattle, leaving Mark behind. Lucas had decided one of them should stay at or near the house at all times. Not that he figured there was much chance of danger by daylight. Still, "Keep Latigo saddled and ready, in among the cottonwoods, at all times," he advised. "If there seems any likelihood of trouble, come for me in a hurry."

So Latigo dozed near the springhouse. And, left alone, Mark kept busy. It was never necessary to hunt work on a ranch. In the course of his chores he moved into the chicken pen to clean it out, and had a look, in passing, at the nests he had fixed up there—not with much hope. He had done a good deal of looking before, with no result.

But this time there was a very pleasant surprise. Mark found two fresh-laid eggs!

He decided on the spot to let everything else go for the time being. He moved into the kitchen, got out flour and lard and sugar and baking powder, arranged mixing bowls, stoked up the stove, and began the job of mixing and baking a cake.

Just before Mark's last birthday, Lucas, on what seemed a routine visit to town, had surprised him with a birthday dinner including a cake with candles on it. Mark had decided then and there Lucas must have a cake for his next birthday, too, made by his son.

It was still several days away, but the eggs couldn't wait and Mark wasn't sure there would be any more. He would bake the cake and hide it in the springhouse, then bring it out as a surprise for Sunday dinner.

Mrs. Harvey, sworn to secrecy, had instructed him, step by step, several times over. It hadn't seemed very difficult then, and Mark had wondered why women made such a fuss about what seemed a pretty simple project.

Now, however, things didn't seem to go the way they had in Mrs. Harvey's kitchen. He spilled flour and had to scoop it up, then forgot how many cups of it he was supposed to use and whether the sugar went in first or the lard for shortening. All of the mixing bowls got filled up and he couldn't remember what was in each of them.

He began to feel exasperated and then anxious, afraid Lucas would walk in on him, with the kitchen beginning to look like a twister had blown through it.

Mark was trying to measure vanilla extract into a teaspoon when the rear door suddenly opened. He started violently, spilling the extract on the floor, and wheeled around—to discover Madge Benteen standing there, staring in amazement at him.

She was wearing her riding gear, the loop of a quirt over one wrist. Madge stared—and began to laugh. She put a hand over her mouth, with a sputtering sound coming through her fingers. She groped for a chair and sat down.

She looked at him again and went into another gale of merriment.

"Stop it!" Mark yelled furiously. "Doggone it, stop laughing at me!"

He was upset not only by her amusement, but also because he had been so absorbed by the effort to get the infernal cake mixed and in the oven that he hadn't even heard her approaching. Anybody at all could have walked in on him.

"I'm s-sorry!" Madge gasped. "But I can't h-help it. You've got flour on your face and on your clothes and in your hair. And lard too!" She wiped her eyes, then sobered a little. "My goodness, Mark, what are you up to, anyway?"

There was no other way out, he had to tell her, or she would think he was just plain crazy. So Mark explained, and Madge did no more laughing.

Instead, coming to her feet again, she reassured him. "I've fixed lots of cakes. I'll fix this one for you. Get me something I can use for an apron—"

"No!" he said. "I've got to do this myself. Don't you understand? I've just got to!"

"Well . . . but it shouldn't hurt if I just sort of look on and let you know whether you're doing things right,"

Madge said. And, "Please, Mark!"

He hesitated, but only for a moment. It was clear that having a hand in baking the cake was all at once of great importance to Madge. Perhaps she was thinking of her own father and of how it would be if she could do the same for his birthday.

"I guess it will be all right if you do that," he decided gruffly.

Things went a lot better, then. Madge sifted and measured and poured while Mark did the beating, using a big wooden spoon.

While they worked, she told him how Judge Hanavan had invited her to use one of his saddle mounts any time she wished. Madge had decided to pay the McCains a visit.

"It's still the same in that town, not many people wanting to be friends because of my name," she said with some bitterness. "I just had to talk to somebody!"

"Has your father gotten in touch with your mother yet?" Mark asked.

Madge's head was bent for a moment, and he thought she wasn't going to answer the question. But at last, "No. There hasn't been any word at all from him to Mamma," Madge said.

It seemed strange to Mark. But perhaps Trav Benteen hadn't been able to find a way to send a message. Also, his outlaw raids indicated he was constantly on the move.

They poured the batter into the pans and placed the pans in the oven. Mark got out the powdered sugar which Mrs. Harvey had brought him and went to work on the icing for the cake. This was an easier job.

Madge said, watching him, "If we could only have a party! You and Uncle Lucas, Mamma and me—"

"That would be great," Mark agreed. "If you could get a buggy again and bring her out on Sunday. . . ."

Madge's head tipped down once more. "We'll see, Mark. But I don't know whether you'll want us—then. . . ."

It was a remark which didn't seem to make much sense. The girl ought to know she and her mother were always welcome, Mark thought. But then the pans had to come out of the oven, and he didn't have time to ask why she thought anything would have changed by Sunday.

When the cake at last had its icing on, they both stood back and looked at it.

"Mark, it's beautiful!" Madge exclaimed.

Mark thought so too. He was pretty pleased with himself, with the feeling he had accomplished something unusual, even though Madge had helped a lot and he was ready to give her full credit. He hoped Lucas would feel pleased too.

The cake, three layers high, covered with its white icing, sat on a platter. Mark had tested some pan scrapings and had discovered it tasted pretty good too.

"I'll take it out to the springhouse now," he decided.

Madge thought it ought to sit awhile, first. Mark finally agreed to put it in a corner on the back porch, covered by a cloth. Lucas wasn't likely to notice it there.

They cleaned up the kitchen. With that finished, Madge said, "Now can we go for a ride?"

Mark hesitated. Lucas had been gone for a couple of hours and was due back, even somewhat overdue. The afternoon had moved along, so it was now a little past four. Mark decided that as long as he kept the house in sight it wouldn't do any harm to ride with Madge a bit; he would watch for Lucas and hurry back so the cake could be moved before his father was on hand.

They went out together. It was a drowsy, warm sort of afternoon, the horses standing sleepily in the corral, the sky a cloudless blue. There was nobody at all in sight, no telltale haze of dust showing above the road from town to indicate that riders might be approaching.

Madge's horse was a small, mettlesome claybank which did an eager dance step as she approached it. The girl swung expertly into saddle and reined the horse back and forth several times across the yard to show off its paces. Then she followed Mark, who was heading toward the springhouse.

Her brows lifted in surprise at the sight of Latigo tethered there, the blankets spread to air on the ground. But she made no comment. Mark said, "I guess we can take a turn toward the east line and then come back."

It was fun to ride with someone who liked horses and the handling of them as much as he did. They let their mounts out a little, matching strides on a run through the high grass, then reined them down again. This was no race, but just a burst of speed because it was exciting.

They came to an east-line marker, one of a series of whitewashed rocks which Lucas had set to indicate the ranch boundary line. Mark stopped there and pointed to the land they hoped to acquire later on. Lucas had bought a full section to start with—a square mile of grass—and was planning to add more, a quarter-section at a time, as soon as the money was available.

They would own that now-unused land in time, Mark told himself—some day, when the troubles bothering them now were finished. And those troubles had to end soon, just had to; he mustn't let himself think of the possibility that the McCains might be driven from what they now owned—and lose everything.

He looked toward the house, still saw no one in sight. Lucas had not reappeared. A glance toward the south did not reveal him either. "I guess we'd better get back," Mark said, turning Latigo.

A moment later he heard the crack of the quirt which Madge carried but had not yet used, heard the claybank whinny in startled protest, then fast hoofbeats as the horse leaped into a run.

Mark looked around. Madge was driving the claybank away from him as fast as it would move—north, toward the thick timber along the river.

He yelled, "No! Not that way! Come back!"

Lucas had told him, before, to keep Madge away from the dark tangles along the river. He knew the order was still in force, that there were many reasons why the girl should not go there.

Madge did not answer or look around. She swung the

quirt again, and her mount responded with an added burst of speed.

Mark had no choice but to heel Latigo hard and go after her—the second time, he reminded himself angrily, that he had been forced to pursue the girl. And what was the reason for the way she was behaving this time?

It took only a minute or so to indicate Latigo had no chance of catching up, heading her off. The claybank had too much of a lead. They hit some rough country this side of the timber, then a marshy spot with pools where the river had overflowed in its last spring flood. Madge did not slacken speed, but drove straight across.

Mark guided Latigo around the pools. There was no use in them being splashed also. About all he could hope for was to rejoin her among the thickly ranked cottonwoods and willows along the south bank of the river, get hold of her horse's reins, and take her back to the house whether she wanted to go or not.

Maybe, he thought, she just wanted a look at the river there and, in her headstrong way, had gone to take that look. This didn't sound like much of an explanation for the way she was behaving, but Mark couldn't think of another one.

But there was another reason—a powerful and frightening one—which had brought Madge Benteen here today. Only a moment or so later Mark discovered what it was.

The girl had halted the claybank, in among the trees, and was looking around. She called, "Papa! I'm here! I came like you told me to."

The hairs at the back of Mark's neck seemed to stand straight out. She had come to meet her father!

He looked hurriedly around. The river murmured placidly in its wide sandy bed, sparkling in the hot sunlight. It was deeply quiet here. There wasn't even the faintest of breezes to stir the thick greenery of the trees.

But Mark had a sense of danger, deadly and immediate. Because Travis Benteen might be close by—and Sid Cade with him.

He wasn't afraid of Madge's father. Cade was something different.

Madge called out again, now with a note of desperation in her voice: "Papa, answer me! Please!"

Mark sent Latigo at the claybank, then. The feeling of fear had lasted only for a second. It was gone now, as the quiet persisted, to be replaced by anger directed at Madge.

Everything she had done this afternoon, he told himself,

had been planned for this moment. She hadn't really been interested in helping him with the cake. All she had wanted was to come to this place—and had used him to accomplish that.

He leaned to pull the claybank's reins from her hands. "Come on, Madge. We're going back." He made an effort to keep his voice from being rough, but did not succeed very well.

Madge looked at him. "Mark, I didn't fib to you, honestly I didn't. My mother didn't receive any message. I did. And I had to do as it said!"

Her face was very pale, her eyes wide and pleading. Something rustled in the high, thick brush nearby, but it was only a cottontail rabbit, popping into the open and then darting away.

"I could have come straight here by myself," Madge went on. "I tried to. But there were some men here then —and Papa said he would be alone. I don't think they saw me. I backed off and went to your place. It seemed I couldn't meet Papa, not today, and I was glad to help you with the cake, because it gave me something to think about. . . ."

She must have been under considerable mental strain,

Mark thought, his anger fading. And—some men here. Had Madge almost stumbled on the members of Benteen's bunch?

"Then, with Uncle Lucas gone, I knew I had to try again—and get you to come along," Madge said. "So if those men were still here, we could pretend that we were just out for a ride."

He wasn't angry at all now. Mark felt deep pity for Madge Benteen. If the situation were different, if he were trying to find Lucas, Mark knew he would do just about anything, also, to accomplish that.

But now, tugging on the claybank's reins, he urged, "We have to go back—he isn't here—"

"No!" Madge protested. "I must wait. He said he'd make it, some time today. I know Papa will keep his promise!"

"Right, daughter. I have," a deep, uneven voice said from behind them.

Mark swung around.

Travis Benteen had come out of a thicket of vines and thorny buckbrush, and even thornier wild blackberry tangles. He looked worn and tired, with dark hollows under his eyes. His once fancy gear, dirty and tattered, hung on him loosely. The lawless life he had been leading had obviously been very hard on him.

But there was a tough, indomitable purpose in the man as he studied Mark for a moment. "Sit steady on that horse, son. Don't make any move at all."

Then his attention shifted to Madge, and his mouth began to work loosely. "Honey, you've grown so much!"

She cried out wordlessly, twisting in saddle, leaping down, running to him with her arms lifted.

Mark felt as though there was a hard cold lump right in the pit of his stomach. Who were the men Madge had sighted earlier—and what was going to happen next?

12   With Bullets Flying!

Mark sat quite still on Latigo, holding the claybank's reins. The quiet continued, here in this peaceful, cool stretch of timber by the river—not so quiet that he could hear what Travis Benteen was telling his daughter nearby in a hurried rush of words—but then, Mark felt no desire to eavesdrop on them.

They had been separated for years. Their reunion should be private. He looked away from them.

Mark felt his own tension lessening. There was nothing in sight to cause any worry. It was going to be all right, he thought hopefully. Benteen would go away and Mark would ride back with Madge. She would return to town. No one would have to know about the meeting here.

Except Lucas, of course. Lucas must be told. It would then be up to his father as to whether Micah should be informed of this secret place.

Madge's voice was suddenly raised: "Papa, I—I don't know whether I ought to tell Mamma that, or whether she will do it—"

"It's the only chance we have of being together again, Madge," Benteen said. "You must make her do it!"

Then they started talking softly again.

Mark shifted position in saddle. He found himself wondering what Lucas was doing, what it was that had kept his father away for so long.

A moment later Latigo's ears began to move back and forth. He stamped the ground gently.

Mark felt his heart leap into his throat. He knew every mood of his pony, knew what the little horse was trying to tell him.

He twisted again to look toward Benteen. The outlaw, head bent, still talking to Madge, did not notice.

Mark wrestled briefly with himself, whether to speak out or stay silent.

And he had to speak, because of Madge. He just couldn't have her in the way here if there were going to be trouble.

"Somebody's coming!" Mark called softly.

Benteen reacted instantly, head snapping up, gun leaping from holster into his hand. He gave Madge a hard thrust. "Get her away from here, boy!" Then he was running, back into the thicket from which he had emerged.

A man shouted, somewhere nearby, frighteningly close. Brush crackled as horses were spurred through it. Riders were driving toward this spot from both directions along the bank.

Trav Benteen came out of the thicket again, this time sitting the big black that Mark remembered from their first meeting. He spun the horse around, indecisive for a moment. Guns were beginning to bark.

Madge was standing as though frozen. Benteen turned his black horse and drove straight for the river.

The shouting was growing louder, closer, and at least a dozen guns were roaring. Mark slid out of saddle and ran at Madge. He slammed her unceremoniously flat against the ground and crouched beside her. "Stay down!"

Horsemen poured out of the trees, all about them. Mark had a glimpse of Micah Torrance, his right arm stiff against his side. Micah sent a single hard glance his way, then called, "He's in the river, heading for the north bank!"

They wheeled and pounded away. Micah's new deputy, Pete Nader, was riding with him.

Mark rose again. He gave Madge his hand, helping her up. "We'd better stay here—" he began.

She paid him no heed, running toward the riverbank.

The guns were roaring again, all along that bank. Mark, following the girl, saw Micah's posse strung out in a line. He saw Benteen in the river.

Madge's father had moved very fast in his effort to escape. He had reached the deep part of the river. His horse was swimming, strongly, angling a little downstream. Benteen had slid back out of saddle, was holding on to the horn. Only his horse's head and his own head were visible.

Bullets were spouting in the water, from the men who were emptying their guns, but they were all short. Benteen was at least a hundred yards away and was increasing that distance every moment—distance much too great for effective accuracy with a handgun. Even a couple of men with rifles were falling short. Micah shouted, "Get your sights up!"

Then Mark saw Lucas standing on the bank.

It was a startling discovery. Where had he come from? How long had he been here? And—had he known of Benteen's meeting with Madge before the posse's arrival?

Lucas was holding the rifle with both hands, half-raised.

Micah's tough deputy became aware of him also and shouted, "Use it!"

All of the guns fell silent as the other men discovered Lucas there. The deputy shouted again, "Use it—or prove you're hand in glove with him!"

Lucas' face was more hard, his brow more ridged, than anything Mark had ever seen before. The rifle lifted, a little.

Madge cried out, incoherently, and covered her face with both hands.

Mark knew his father's amazing marksmanship. He knew that, even at the distance Benteen had now gained, Lucas might miss with one bullet, maybe even with two. But then, with his sights adjusted, he could not possibly miss a third time. Lucas could surely stop Benteen before the man could ever gain the north bank.

The hardwood stock was almost against Lucas' shoulder before he lowered the rifle and turned away.

A sort of muttering sigh of disbelief and anger seemed to ripple through the men who made up Micah's posse. Then they were silent, watching as Benteen's horse emerged on the opposite side, made a run across a sandbar and up the bank. There Benteen turned, with a lift of his hand, before he rode in among the trees and disappeared.

A moment later Pete Nader, the tough deputy, was facing Lucas, jaw thrust out, eyes hot and angry. "So it's true!" he said furiously. "You've been lending him help all along—you and your sneaky kid!"

Lucas put down the rifle. His fist flashed at the man's jaw, an incredibly fast blow, snapped straight from the shoulder. It had the sound, as it hit, of Lucas' double-bitted axe chunking into wood.

The deputy's feet seemed to fly from under him. He hit the ground hard on his back and sprawled there for a moment, motionless. Lucas scooped up his rifle and made a partial turn toward the others. He did not speak, did not have to do so. The gesture was a warning that it would not be advisable for anyone else to repeat what one deputy had said.

The man scrambled shakily up. Hand to jaw, he shouted at Micah, "Well, what are you waiting for? Haul him in —the kid too. . . . I'll guarantee Benteen won't be breaking them out of jail!"

Micah, the seams showing deeply in his face, said, "No, Pete. I've told you before that I'll handle this my way, not yours." Then, including all of them, "Back on your horses.

We've got to follow Benteen across the river, try to run him down—"

"Not me!" Nader snapped. "I'm heading straight to town—where I mean everybody to know what happened here, with advice that what North Fork needs is a new marshal, one who'll deal with these McCains—and who won't let Benteen get away every time he shows himself!"

"You'll recommend yourself for my job, no doubt?" Micah asked.

"Yes!" the deputy said.

"Well, I can't stop you from making your try—but I can fire you for disobeying an order," Micah said. "Take off that badge."

The deputy, lip curling, ripped the badge from his shirt and threw it in the dirt at Micah's feet. He turned and stamped away. The possemen were exchanging glances. One after another, four of them left the group, mounted up, and followed Pete Nader off along the bank toward North Fork.

The rest swung into saddle and headed down to the river for the crossing and the taking up again of the chase after Travis Benteen—and with the lead he had gained, it seemed probable that would be hopeless.

Micah and Lucas were left, facing each other.

Lucas spoke first. "I want Trav caught as much as you do, Micah, but I couldn't pull trigger, not with him helpless in the river. I just couldn't!"

"I know," Micah said. "If you'll remember, I wasn't the one yelling at you to shoot. But the fact that you didn't, sure makes things a lot tougher."

"For you, as well as for me," Lucas agreed. "I'm sorry that I gave that loud mouth, Nader, a club to use against you."

Micah shrugged. "I can stand losing my job—can always pick up another one," he said. "But you're liable to lose everything, Lucas. . . ."

Deep worry showed in his tired features. "A couple of fellows are plaguing me to bring you in, claiming you shot them with no reason—"

"It was trespass!" Lucas snapped. "They came at Mark and me by night. I warned them off, let them have the first shot!"

"Don't you think I figured all that for myself? I know they're lying," Micah said, "and have been able to hold them off, so far. If Nader talks the town into handing him my badge, though, his first act will be to arrest you. And once you're behind bars, in jail. . . ."

Micah did not finish the sentence. It was not necessary. If Lucas were put in jail, the charge of working with Benteen's bunch would also be lodged against him.

He would be behind bars, with the ranch wide open for whatever vengeful action those night riders might choose to take against him.

"There's reason to hope none of that will ever happen, Micah—plenty of levelheaded people in town, who see things straight," Lucas said.

"Plenty of the other kind, too, unfortunately, enough to vote me out of my job," Micah said. "I'm scared, Lucas, plenty scared, that if Benteen and his whole bunch aren't caught soon—"

He left another sentence unfinished, bent to pick up the deputy's badge from the dirt, then went and climbed on his horse, with some difficulty, because of his hurt arm. His possemen were strung out in the river, making the crossing to the north bank.

Micah had something more to say, with a glance to Madge, who was still standing beside Mark. "I've had that girl watched, too, along with her mother—followed her out here today with the guess she might be trying to meet her father. Guessed, too, it would be somewhere along the river—got ahead of her and hunted at least five miles through the tangles; he must have hid himself real good. Then I was turning back, giving up, when suddenly she was here with Mark—and with Benteen."

At those words Lucas, tight-lipped, sent a look at Mark.

"Split my men and hit from both directions," Micah went on. "I thought I had him, sure. But he was both lucky and clever. . . ."

He glanced toward Madge. "Lucas, see to it, any way necessary, that she stays in town after this! My blood was running cold, her and Mark there; with bullets flying!"

The marshal rode down to the river, then, and into it.

They headed back, Lucas in the middle, Madge on one side of him, Mark on the other. Razor had been left at some distance; Lucas had gone to get the black and had waited on them.

There was no talk. Lucas seemed lost in his grim thoughts, Mark didn't feel like saying anything, and what Madge might be thinking he couldn't begin to guess.

Until they reached the house, at least, when Lucas said quietly, "Madge, you'd better go right on to town," and

Mark noticed tears on the girl's cheeks.

She had been through an awful lot, he realized, first the meeting with her father, after being so long apart, and then those terrible moments when bullets were flying at him. Mark wished there were something he could do or say that would ease things a little for Madge.

But she nodded jerkily, in obedience to what amounted to an order. "Uncle Lucas, I—I'm very sorry that I've caused you and Mark so much trouble—"

"It's all right," Lucas said gently. "Give my best regards to your mother."

She rode away, bringing a moment Mark had dreaded, when he must face Lucas alone and try to explain.

He made the attempt. Lucas heard him out with no comment. Then, however, "You knew the danger that might be there—for Madge, and also for yourself. You should have stopped her from going to that river timber, using any means necessary."

"She got a lead on me," Mark reminded him. "She got there first."

"Then you should have made her come back, as soon as you caught up with her," Lucas said.

Mark had tried to make Madge return—but not as soon

as he caught up. He remembered how she had started talking, how he had waited a minute or so, listening to her, before making his try to pull the claybank away.

But he wasn't going to refer to that. It would sound as though he were offering an excuse, and Lucas had taught him that a man stood by his actions, taking the consequences for them if he was wrong, without making any excuses. In that instance, at least, not acting quickly enough to make Madge leave, he had been wrong.

"Yes, sir," Mark said. "I'm sorry."

"Mark, those two words, 'I'm sorry,' are the easiest in the English language to say," Lucas told him. "And saying them, with a notion they take care of everything, is a mighty bad habit, one I don't want you to acquire."

"Yes, sir," Mark said. "I won't."

"Let's get along inside now," Lucas continued. "I'm going to eat an early supper and try for a nap before dark."

It seemed to Mark that things got worse, during the next half hour or so, instead of better.

He tried several times to get talk started, but Lucas was not responsive. Then Mark gave thought to his father's grim preoccupation with the dark threat which hung over both of them and decided to keep quiet. Thinking about it, he began to feel pretty grim also.

They moved about in the kitchen, Mark spreading the tablecloth and setting the places while Lucas prepared the meal. Working at this, Lucas went onto the back porch several times for various things.

A sudden startled exclamation from him, during one of those trips, brought Mark out also. He saw Lucas standing in the corner, with the cloth lifted from the cake, staring down at it, then at him, and Mark felt his heart sink right into his boots.

With so much else, he had forgotten all about the cake and taking it to the springhouse.

"It—it's a birthday cake, Pa," he faltered. "For you. I baked it. Well, Madge helped me. I meant it for a surprise —have some candles Mrs. Harvey gave me—"

Then he seemed to run out of words.

Lucas did not say anything either. His face was complete-ly lacking in expression. Maybe a minute passed, certainly the longest minute of Mark's life.

It ended in surprising fashion. Lucas let the cloth down on the cake again. He turned and opened the screen door. He stepped through it, let the door close quietly behind him, and walked across the yard.

Mark did not know what to do. Presently he took the cake into the kitchen and put it on the table. Lucas had once said there were times when every man had a need to be alone and his right to that should be respected. Maybe this was one of those times.

He waited in the kitchen. It was beginning to grow dark. After a while Mark went hesitantly out the rear door.

Lucas was standing by the corral. He looked around and nodded, with a smile, as Mark came slowly along.

"I've been standing here and thinking—about the hardest job a man ever has to tackle," Lucas said. "Do you know what that is, Mark?"

"No, sir," Mark replied.

"It's the job of being a father," Lucas told him. "You'll find out, some day—how you have no experience to guide you, but must learn everything as you go along, making mistakes, feeling bad about them. . . . I made a mistake a while ago, son."

Mark looked down at his boots. His throat felt tight, maybe because of something very quiet and deep in his father's voice that he had never heard there before.

"I was all wrapped up in worry about our troubles, so

wrapped up I wouldn't talk—and after we agreed a long time ago that we'd never let anything turn us silent on each other," Lucas said. "When I saw that cake and realized all you must have gone through to fix it—well, I was hit pretty hard. I apologize, son."

"Gosh, you don't need to do that, Pa," Mark protested. "I understand—with all those troubles—"

"Which we'll face together, the way it should be, as a team, side by side!" Lucas said. "I almost lost sight of that for a little while, Mark. I'm glad you reminded me."

Then he laughed, putting an arm about his son's shoulders. "Come on, now, let's go in and cut that cake! I can't wait!"

"But I've got to put the candles on!" Mark began.

Lucas laughed again, starting him toward the house. "Never mind the candles! I told you I can't wait. Anyway, I don't need them to make me feel any better than I am now—standing ten feet tall, with you for a son, and nothing at all ahead of us that we can't handle!"

13   A Desperate Plan

Next day Mark found out why Lucas had been away for so long the previous afternoon. His father had found a break in the south fence where some of the older cattle had butted at a post until it broke off. A couple of strands of wire had snapped and half a dozen head had slipped through the break and headed for open country, the way they always would, given half a chance.

Lucas had rounded them up and driven them back, then closed the gap with some brush. They rode to handle the job of mending it.

"Good thing now we got that reel of wire," Lucas remarked. "I'll cut a couple of new posts while you start digging the holes, Mark."

It was hard, sweaty work, but Mark found it enjoyable. He and Lucas took off their shirts to get a tan, though being good cattlemen, they kept their hats on. Mark had the holes dug by the time Lucas found a cottonwood sapling of the right size, cut it down, and chopped out and trimmed two posts of the right length. Two were needed to make the fence stronger, with one bracing the other.

There was the job, then, of unreeling the wire, measuring and cutting it, stapling it into place—the whole job representing another of the skills that a cattleman had to know and know well, if he were to run a successful ranch.

And everything went as though this were just another day—as though Lucas had not stayed up the whole previous night again, on guard with the rifle.

Mark had tried to stay awake, too, so as to offer help if it were needed, but he had drifted off to sleep in spite of that. He worked doubly hard today to make up for his inability to keep his eyes open.

Lucas whistled softly as they stretched and stapled the wire, concentrating completely on the job as though it were the only thing that mattered in the world. This puzzled Mark a little. It seemed to him that, with so much which was unpleasant perhaps about to happen, Lucas should act more worried.

When they had finished the job and were admiring the

now strong fence, he diffidently mentioned this. Lucas shook his head.

"I've told you before, son, there's never anything to be gained by borrowing trouble. And I did some thinking last night. It came clear to me that, though certain things might happen, none of them are to be expected right away."

He tested the tension in the new wire strands and went on, "There's a time element involved. Micah might lose his job to Nader, who then might try to make trouble for us; but neither of those things will happen today."

Mark nodded in understanding. "And those fellows who hit us the other night won't try it again today either."

"That's right. Also, they aren't really very likely to try it again at all if they think there's a chance I'll be put in jail for shooting a couple of them. So we might as well enjoy the sunshine and get some work done."

But he continued to study the fence, whistling again, and after some moments continued, "I've got a strong hunch about something that I think will happen, though —and when . . . . Mark, did you happen to hear anything that Madge and her father talked about, when they met?"

"No, sir," Mark replied. "I didn't think that I ought to try to do any listening."

Lucas nodded in agreement. "I thought they might have raised their voices, not caring whether they were overheard. Well, I've a pretty good idea what it was Trav told her. But it'll require a little time, too, before I find out whether I'm right about that—about what he means to do next."

He said no more on the subject as they mounted and rode back to the house—or later, leaving Mark with a strong itch of curiosity as he tried to figure out just what it was that Lucas expected Benteen to do.

Somewhat later in the day he suddenly realized there might be a clue in the fact Lucas had not done what Micah had asked him to do: He had not told Madge to stay in town. But it was only a clue. It didn't clear things up.

They finished the day with the feeling of a lot accomplished.

Lucas turned in for a nap just before sundown, and Mark let him sleep fairly late, not shaking him awake until a considerable while after dark—meanwhile keeping watch himself. He had noticed a lot of sounds in the night that he had never noticed before, scary sounds, some of them; but he manfully resisted the temptation to wake his father.

Lucas did not comment on the lateness of the hour.

Instead, he murmured, "Into your blankets now, son," and
went away for a quick, silent check on everything nearby:
the house, the barn, the corral, the outbuildings.

But tonight was apparently part of the waiting for things
to happen, because when Mark stirred, sometime later,
and opened a drowsy eye, he saw Lucas sitting nearby, back
against a tree—and he wouldn't be doing that if there was
any feeling in him of danger.

So the night passed, bringing another day and more
matter-of-fact handling of the never-ending round of work.
And, as Lucas had once remarked, if a man didn't like to
work at something, really like it, he had no excuse for
being.

Mark liked to work well enough, though he wished a
garden would grow without requiring so much hoeing. He
was at that, around midmorning, moving as fast as
he could between rows of corn that were getting higher than
he was, when a rider suddenly came along from town,
moving in a considerable hurry.

Mark recognized him from a distance, Dick Barnes, the
young fellow who edited the weekly town newspaper,
the *North Fork Eagle*—which meant he also worked
indirectly for Judge Hanavan and Banker Hamilton, since

they had put up the money to get the paper started.

Lucas came from the barn to greet him. They conferred briefly, the rider leaning down to deliver some message, and then he was gone again, returning at a gallop toward North Fork.

Mark headed for the barn. His father was standing in deep thought. Mark said, offhandedly, "Thought I'd give the grindstone a couple of turns and put an edge on this old hoe. It's getting kind of dull."

Lucas smiled faintly. "Curious about what all that meant, Mark? Well, I can't blame you." Then he was frowning. "Judge Hanavan sent me a message. Benteen's bunch hit again last night—another of the cattlemen, owner of a big herd that came out of the mesa country yesterday afternoon."

"South of town," Mark said.

"Quite a distance south," Lucas said. "Micah and his posse headed that way about an hour ago. If I know Micah, he probably doesn't think much of hunting Benteen in that direction, not after losing him north of the river. Micah must have figured by this time, also, that there's a pattern in what Benteen is doing, and that he's not likely to be caught down toward the mesas. But Micah has no choice, with the town demanding action. He has to ride there and hope for the best."

Lucas began whistling softly again. His eyes were narrowed speculatively. "Curious business, this latest action by Benteen. That cattleman was packing some cash, but only about a thousand dollars, a whole lot less than Trav has been aiming for lately. Also, the cattleman was handed a beating. The town is pretty indignant."

"Maybe," Mark ventured, "Benteen wants Micah and his posse to head in that direction!"

Lucas glanced at him. "You know something, son? I'm thinking that, myself."

"But why should he want such a thing?"

"You'd better go and start the grindstone turning," Lucas said. "I'm of the opinion, too, that the hoe needs a new edge."

So Mark went and worked the grindstone treadle for a while. It was obvious Lucas had a pretty good idea of the explanation of what had happened and what was due to happen next. Mark couldn't figure it out at all.

He finished with the grindstone, which was located in a lean-to behind the barn. Mark walked back through the barn to the yard—to discover Lucas had disappeared.

The barn stood empty and silent. So did the house, and the springhouse. Mark investigated them all. Then he looked every place where Lucas might have left him a note. There was none.

Razor stood drowsing in the corral along with the other horses. Lucas' saddle was on its peg. This made his disappearance even stranger. Lucas, who would work a long day at the toughest job with no complaint, wouldn't walk any distance at all in his tight-fitting, high-heeled boots if there was a horse handy to ride. He was all cattleman in that too.

Mark felt a little frightened. Then he did some reasoning.

Nothing had happened to Lucas—not in broad daylight, while he had the rifle in his hand. If there had been any kind of try at him, Mark would have heard it.

His father had just dropped out of sight, for some very good reason which he couldn't tell Mark. He hadn't gone anywhere, but must be close by right now, maybe in the tall grass where the south pasture began, flattened out, watching the house. Mark was careful not to look toward that grass, not to do any more looking anywhere.

Instead, he went on with his work as though nothing

had happened. He finished his hoeing in the garden, making a good job of it. By then the time was about noon, so he fixed himself some lunch, cold beef and biscuits, which he ate standing up in the kitchen.

Afterward the chores went on, again as though nothing had happened: fresh water for the horses, some work on them with a currycomb. Mark chopped firewood and filled the stove box. He took down the harness and hung it on iron hooks, which had been specially made by Nils Swenson, got out the saddle soap, and began cleaning it.

This was work Mark particularly liked, the good smell of leather and working the foamy lather into it.

The job was not quite done when the sound of a horse moving at a slow walk reached him. He went out of the barn and saw Travis Benteen, leading his big black, coming alongside the irrigation ditch, wading it, stopping to send a look at him, then at the whole place. "Mark, where's your father?"

"I don't know. He went away, before noon. I don't know when he'll be back either."

Benteen relaxed a little. There was a gun in his hand. He put it back in its holster. "I'm glad to hear that, have been dreading that maybe I'd have to tangle with him. Could you give my horse some oats?"

Mark led the black into the barn and scooped feed from the bin. He also spread some hay for the animal, which ate as though it had been on very short rations.

Benteen had followed him and leaned against a stall post, looking on. "Madge told me that you and Lucas have been very kind to her and to my wife, your Aunt Susan. I want to thank you for that."

"I guess we'd have done more, if we could," Mark said.

"Some of those people in that town—she told me about the way they treated them!" the man said bitterly.

It was his fault, the things he had done, which had caused some of the town people to act that way. Mark did not say this, though.

He noticed there was a different saddle on the black, hand-tooled, with silver markings. It also carried some bulging saddlebags, and the reins were fancy, too—all gear for show, not honest use. Mark supposed Travis Benteen had taken it from somebody.

He took hold of the cinch strap, meaning to loosen it, but Benteen said, "No. I don't mean to stay here a minute longer than necessary."

The man paced out in front of the barn, then. As soon

as the horse had eaten its fill, Mark led it out.

Benteen was looking toward town, rubbing his hands together, pulling at his fingers. He seemed even more worn down and tired than two days ago at the river, but with a restless, driving force in him. He was a long way from being worn out.

Mark watched him, with awareness that he was, himself, not at all scared. Perhaps it was because he knew that Lucas must be somewhere close, watching—also because he realized that he had nothing in particular to fear from Benteen. This man who was his uncle did not intend to harm him.

Even more, though, it was because of the way Mark discovered he was feeling about Benteen—and what he felt was pity.

Travis Benteen had done things which some might think exciting and spectacular. Mark didn't think so. They had brought Benteen to this moment, when he was being hunted by many men in many places, as though he were a wolf that had to be caught or shot. He had to be on guard every minute, day and night, because each minute might be his last.

Mark couldn't feel anger at him because of the trouble

he had caused the McCains. Only pity.

Then Benteen exclaimed. A rig had appeared, over the rise just west of the corral on the road to town, and Mark realized that what Lucas had been expecting, waiting for, was about to happen.

It was the same rent rig from the town livery stable which Rufus Dabney had used on his visit here. But this time Madge was handling the reins, and her mother was sitting beside her.

Again, Mark did not feel he should watch as Benteen had his reunion with his wife. He turned and walked away, stood near the barn looking toward the springhouse for a while.

After several minutes Madge came to join him there, touching his arm lightly. "Please don't be angry with me, Mark."

Madge was dressed as she had been that morning, when she and her mother had first visited the ranch, the green suit and high-buttoned shoes with red tassels. Her dark hair was loose and fell to her shoulders.

Madge's face was tight and pale. She knew as well as did Mark the danger of this moment.

"You shouldn't have done it," Mark said. "You shouldn't have come here."

"But it's what Papa told me to do, there at the river," Madge said. "I had to obey him, Mark. We rented the surrey and went for a drive yesterday—and were followed then. But we weren't followed today. I made sure of that. I guess the marshal had to take all of his men with him when he rode away this morning and didn't have anybody to leave behind to watch us."

Micah had probably taken all the men he could trust, or who would still take his orders, Mark thought. But there was Nader, plus the men backing him for Micah's job. Nader might have followed them, in a way Madge couldn't spot.

Benteen called to his daughter, and Madge went back to join him and her mother.

Mark slowly followed along, with a question burning in him: Why wasn't Lucas appearing on the scene, now that what he had waited for was happening?

It was certain Lucas had figured it all out—that Benteen would want to see his wife, also, and that this was the only place it could be done—with something set up to pull Micah and the posse away from town, in the hope Madge and her mother would not be followed.

The attack on the Texas cattleman had been the move to send Micah and his men riding off to the south. Lucas had recognized that that was its meaning, had known it signaled this meeting.

Then why didn't he do something, with Benteen right here?

Travis Benteen was talking fast, not bothering to keep his voice down. It wasn't a question of Mark eavesdropping —unless he put his hands over his ears, he couldn't help hearing what was being said.

"Take the first stage out tomorrow," Benteen was directing his wife. "When you reach Oglalla, get on an eastbound train. Keep riding until you reach New Orleans. That'll take you about a week. Go to the Carondelet Hotel and wait for me. I'll need more time to get there, maybe two weeks, maybe three—"

"And then?" Susan Benteen said. She was even paler than Madge, was standing with her hand on her husband's arm as though badly needing something to cling to for support.

"We'll sail on the first boat for South America— Argentina," Benteen said. "I've got the big stake I've always been working for, enough to buy land, cattle. We'll have our own place, down there."

"Argentina. It—it seems such a long way off," Susan Benteen said faintly.

"It is! Far enough so nobody'll know me, so I can live free—forget about the past and everything in it, build for the future!"

"I suppose we'll have to change our names?" his wife said, with a glance toward Madge.

"Yes. I suppose we will," Benteen muttered. "It'd be too dangerous, otherwise. Somebody might turn up who would remember there was a Benteen that was wanted here—"

The woman looked down at the ground. Mark had a feeling she was almost about to weep. "Couldn't Madge and I go home first for just a little while to say good-by to all our people?"

"No!" Benteen said. "Don't get in touch with them at all. After we're in South America you can write—though you can't tell exactly where we are."

"But that means we'll never see them again—because we can't ever come back!" she protested.

Mark could see that Madge was scared, too, by what her

father was proposing—to go away to a distant country, never see her relatives again, take a new name. Mark felt pity for her, also, deep pity.

Benteen took some money, bank notes, from his pocket and put them in his wife's hand. "This is enough to pay all your expenses. And I can't stay here a minute longer. I'm starting for New Orleans, right now. Do as I say, Susan! It's the only chance on earth for the three of us to be together again!"

"All right, Trav," Susan Benteen said, voice very faint. "I—I'll be in New Orleans, waiting—"

"No, Susan," Lucas McCain said. "You won't."

He had made his appearance at last, walking quietly out of the barn, and Mark realized instantly where he had been all this time—in the hayloft, where he could keep a watchful eye on everything through the outside loading door, so silent there had been no move, no unguarded sound to tell anyone he was there.

"You're not going to do this to them, Trav," Lucas said. "I'm not going to let you do it."

He was holding his rifle at waist level, gripped lightly with both hands—not pointing at Benteen, but the muzzle could whip around at him with lightning speed.

Benteen wheeled a little to face him. Benteen's right hand dropped to the handle of his holstered gun.

"Lucas, don't you make the bad mistake of trying to stop me!" he said.

14   "I'm Riding Out!"

Mark discovered he was holding his breath and standing rigid—but then he discovered this was true of the others also. Their shadows were very black against the ground. It was so quiet that when Latigo suddenly snorted in the corral, the sound seemed as loud as a rifle shot and made him jump.

Susan Benteen held out her hand in a shaky, pleading gesture. "Lucas—don't!" she began.

"Keep quiet, Susan," her husband said, without taking his eyes off Lucas. "I'll handle this. You don't need to do any begging for me."

Lucas' eyes were boring into him also. "I heard everything you told Susan, Trav."

"So?" Benteen said.

"It won't work," Lucas said. "It's the old dream, held

223

sooner or later by every outlaw—to quit the crooked bunch, the crooked life, and get back on the right side of the law, to live free again. But it never comes true. It can't."

"It will for me!" Benteen said.

Lucas shook his head. "The world isn't big enough. There's no place far enough away that somebody won't recognize you, remember your name, come at you with a gun, either for the rewards on your head or to grab what you're taking with you—or both. Or else the law will come after you, in Argentina or anywhere."

Benteen's face was dark now as he thought of what Lucas had said. Not that he was convinced, or even close to it. Mark feared that nothing Lucas could say was going to convince him.

"And give some thought to Susan and Madge," his father went on. "They'll have to begin new lives, in a strange country—with the knowledge that any hour, or any minute, they might be alone again, far from home—"

"That isn't going to happen!" Benteen said.

He suddenly shifted position, moving a little to one side, and Mark's heart skipped a beat with the realization Benteen was putting the sun at his back, and in Lucas' eyes.

Lucas didn't seem to notice what the man was doing.

He still held the rifle loosely. His finger was not yet on its trigger ring.

"I'm leaving, now," Benteen said. "Don't try to stop me, Lucas."

"Leaving with your share of the loot taken by you and your bunch?" Lucas said. "I've noticed those full saddle-bags on your horse—"

"I've quit the bunch," Benteen said. "They're on their own now. And they did all right too."

"You won't reconsider—about this plan to go away with Susan and Madge?"

"You heard me tell them; we'll all meet in New Orleans. That's not going to be changed!"

"You won't quit for that reason, then," Lucas said. "But there's another one—the harm you've done me and Mark —even more, the harm you still can do. . . ."

Benteen's brow ridged for a moment. "I thought for a while, at the start, that I could force you to throw in with me. We'd have made a great team, the two of us! But that didn't work out. Now—just what harm can I do you by pulling out, for good?"

Lucas told him of the belief held by some that he had been helping Travis Benteen.

"That'll be quick forgotten!" Benteen said.

"Not if I let you get away with what you're planning. Talk will soon start—that I helped you to the last, helped you make your start at leaving the country. That will be the final blow. Mark and I can't live here any longer. We'll be lucky if we're even given the chance to leave too."

"What do you want from me?" Benteen demanded. "Anybody would think, the way you're talking, that you have in mind I should give up, let them put me behind bars!"

"That's exactly what I do mean," Lucas said.

Susan Benteen cried out, both hands rising to cover her mouth, and Madge made some dismayed sound too. As for Travis Benteen, his face turned as hard as granite, and his eyes narrowed so they could hardly be seen.

"You owe a debt that has to be paid, Trav," Lucas said. "And paid by you—not by Susan and Madge living in hiding for the rest of their lives."

Benteen said, over his shoulder, "Susan, don't miss that stage to Oglalla tomorrow." Then, "Lucas, I'm riding out."

"It probably won't take as long as you may fear to square yourself," Lucas said. "Five years, certainly no more than ten, especially if you show you want to turn over a new leaf. Then you'd be free, nothing against you, ready to start a new life. With plenty ready to help, including me."

"I know you're fast with that rifle," Benteen said. "I'm fast with this six-gun, too—don't want to use it against you, Lucas, but I will—if you make any move at all."

Lucas made no reply. It had abruptly come to the time when there would be no more talk. Benteen meant to leave. Lucas meant to stop him. Mark realized, as the two men waited, each on the other, each with iron determination evident in his manner, that Lucas must use the rifle. There was no other way.

But there was. A long moment stretched out, in dead silence—then was broken when Sid Cade laughed.

He had come around a corner of the barn and was standing there, a little behind Lucas. Benteen was facing partially away from Cade. Neither he nor Lucas was in a position to do anything. And Cade had a gun gripped in his right fist.

There was wicked amusement in his laugh. "I'd like to wait, just to watch you two finish each other off, which would probably happen," he said. "But I'm in a hurry."

His gun swung menacingly in a slow arc, back and forth. "Don't either of you even wiggle, or I'll start using bullets.

At this distance, I couldn't miss. And it would be a pleasure!"

He had made his approach with the stealth and quiet of a stalking coyote, had caught all of them completely by surprise—including Lucas, who had been concentrating all of his attention on Benteen.

Lucas glanced around at him. He said, voice coldly quiet, "What do you want here, Cade?"

"I want what's in Benteen's saddlebags." The man came a couple of steps closer. "Never cared for his split-up of what we took—half to him, the other half divided between the rest of us. So now I'm taking his half. As simple as that."

Benteen trembled. His lips writhed, though no sound came. The prospect of losing all he had counted on for the flight to South America, the big stake he had worked for in his lawless career, was hitting him as hard as a bullet from Cade's gun.

"Take your right hand off that rifle, McCain," Sid Cade ordered. "Throw it aside with your left hand."

Lucas obeyed him. The rifle slid along the ground.

"Your turn now, Benteen," Cade said. "Reach across for your gun with your left hand—reach slow! Now,

throw it over beside the rifle."

Benteen had the same choice as Lucas, none at all. He obeyed also.

Susan Benteen made a moaning sound. Madge started to move toward her. Cade snapped, "Stand still, girl!"

Madge stopped. Then Cade turned his attention to Mark, who felt the impact of his cold, almost colorless eyes. "Go pick up the gun and the rifle, boy. Bring them to me. And handle them real careful!"

Mark glanced toward his father. A slight jerk of Lucas' head told him to do it. He went to pick up the two weapons on the ground, his legs feeling numb, and carried them to Cade.

The man accepted Benteen's gun first, thrusting it under his belt. Then he reached for the rifle with a grunt of satisfaction. "I've been wanting that, from the first moment I saw it!"

The rifle went under his left arm. Mark started backing away from him.

"You're not going to get away with it!" Benteen said, his voice harsh, strained.

Cade laughed again. "I've had you figured from the moment you found out your wife and daughter were in that town, Benteen—knew just the stunt you'd try. All I had to do was follow along when you decided to cut loose from me and those others. Get away with it? I always finish what I start!"

"I'll be right behind you," Benteen said, "no matter where you go!"

"Trav, shut up!" Lucas snapped.

"That's right good advice," Cade said. "You'd better listen to him, Benteen!"

He hesitated, then, chewing at his lip, while the gun quivered nervously in his fist.

"Could just stick a bullet in each of you two," Cade went on. "That'd be the easiest way to insure neither one of you would be coming after me. But no sense stirring up the whole country, and a shooting would sure do that—"

He sent another look at Mark, who shivered, but inside, where he hoped it wouldn't show. And then Cade's glance shifted away from him—to Madge. And the man said, "You, girl—come here."

It was so still and quiet again for a moment that Mark was sure everybody must be able to hear the thudding of his heart. To Mark, it seemed to be beating like a tom-tom.

Cade gestured with the gun. "I told you . . . come here!"

Madge moved slowly to stand facing him.

"I heard your pa bragging you're a pretty good rider," Cade said. "Gather the reins of his horse and get up on it. Boy, you lend her a hand."

Mark had the feel of moving in a bad dream as he helped Madge rise to the saddle. Her skirt hampered her some, of course, but not much. She adjusted it. She looked down to Mark and tried to smile, as though to tell him she was not afraid.

"Now, listen good," Cade said. "She's going to ride with me a spell. When and where I turn her loose depends on you two. If I'm not followed, she can be back here before dark."

He began to back away. "Come along, girl. McCain, my horse is by your springhouse. You and Benteen stay rooted right where you are. I'll plug anybody that tries to come around the barn after me."

He continued to move, Benteen's black pacing with him.

As they disappeared, Benteen took a lunging step after them. Lucas leaped to grip him with both hands, restraining Madge's father. "Stand still!"

Benteen struggled wildly against him. "Let me go!"

"Can you help her by getting yourself shot?" Lucas snapped. "That's what is sure to happen if you don't heed what he said!"

Benteen stopped struggling, then. They waited. And only a moment or so later a rapid drumming of hoofbeats began, fading away toward the east.

Susan Benteen cried out. She sank to the ground and huddled there, her hands covering her face, weeping brokenly.

Mark hurried to help her up. So did Lucas and her husband. They got her into the surrey.

Benteen turned to Lucas, then. "I want a gun and a horse. I'm going to run him down!"

"Take it easy, Trav," Lucas said. "We're both going after him—but not in any wild rush. We'll have to pack some supplies, grub and water, because we don't know how long a chase it will be. Also, we must let him build up a lead. He'll be edgiest during the first couple of hours, watching his back trail all the time. If he doesn't see anybody following him, maybe he'll do as he said and turn Madge loose."

Lucas tugged at Benteen's arm then and they moved off to one side, where they conferred briefly in low tones.

Benteen's face was drawn and haggard, Lucas' face tight and purposeful, more purposeful than Mark had ever seen it.

Then Lucas said, "Mark!" and he, going to join them, answered, "Yes, sir?"

"You drive your Aunt Susan back to town," his father directed. "Take her to the Madera House; it's the best place for her to be. Turn that rig in at the livery stable. After that—well, I think you had better spend the night with the Harveys."

He paused a moment, thinking hard, and added, "If Judge Hanavan or Mr. Hamilton are in town, tell them what has happened and that nobody is to come after us, that we two must handle this alone if it is to be handled at all."

The last glimpse Mark had of them, as he turned the surrey and rein-slapped its team, heading off along the road, they were hurrying together toward the house, there to gather the things they would need for the trailing of Sid Cade.

His Aunt Susan was very quiet on the fairly rapid run to town. She had stopped weeping, sat with hands clasped tightly in her lap, looking down at them, apparently not very aware of Mark beside her, or of anything else except her grief.

For his part, he was remembering the fortitude Madge had shown, wondering if he would have been able to display the same courage. Mark hoped so. He also knew that he wasn't going to be very good company for himself if he didn't do something to help her, rather than just sitting and waiting at the Harveys.

When he halted the surrey in front of the Madera House, Susan Benteen stirred and spoke, low-voiced, "Thank you, Mark. You're very kind, like Lucas. I don't know why you should be, the trouble we've caused you—but bless you for it!"

She went inside then. And only about an hour later, still short of sundown, Mark was back at the ranch, riding a horse borrowed at the livery stable, which he turned in at the corral. Then he saddled Latigo, made a bundle of his own with what grub he could find in the kitchen, filled a canteen, and started riding again.

The ranch was wholly undefended now, open to anybody who might come along. There wasn't a lock on the place. Nobody would dream of locking a door in this

country, where the latchstring was always out. But what
happened to the ranch did not seem very important right
now.

Picking up the trail left by his father and Travis Benteen
wasn't difficult. You had to learn to read and follow sign
if you were to find cattle that were hiding from you in
the brush. This was easier than that, since Mark knew the
pattern of Razor's shoes as well as he knew the shape of
his own hand.

He also knew Benteen was riding the pinto. He even
spotted, occasionally, the hoofmarks left by Cade and
Madge, which Lucas and Benteen were following.

The direction they were all going was east for a while,
then a sharp angle toward the south. Mark found himself
out on the broad plain where he had followed Madge that
other time; but before long he was in a part of it where he
had never been before, with Latigo constantly scrambling
in and out of fairly deep arroyos.

Mark held the little horse to a steady pace. The sun set
and there was gray twilight for a while. Then the stars
were out, and he wasn't able to follow the trail by sight any
longer.

It seemed he would have to stop and make some sort of

camp for the night, go on just as soon as it was light enough to see clearly. But Latigo nickered and began working his ears. Mark gave the horse its head.

About ten minutes later, he saw them, down in one of the arroyos. The two horses were standing wearily, saddles off. Lucas was sitting on a boulder, quietly eating. Benteen was pacing back and forth.

Lucas came to his feet as Mark guided Latigo down to join them. "What are you doing here?" There was an edge in his voice, but of strain, not anger.

Mark said, "Judge Hanavan wasn't in town. Neither was Mr. Hamilton. I told Nils Swenson; he said he'd spread the word. . . ."

And now the explanation of why he had followed along. Not to deliver that message, since it wasn't really necessary —and not with any notion he might miss some excitement either. Remembering the cold, scary feeling he got whenever Sid Cade was even in sight, it would have been a lot easier and a good deal more comfortable to stay safely in town.

He burst out: "Let me ride with you! I'm worried about Madge too—scared for her. I won't get in the way, will stay back when you tell me to. Maybe the chance will come for me to do something to help. But I just can't wait and not do anything!"

Benteen had stopped pacing to listen. He muttered, "Lucas, let him come along."

Lucas did not say anything for a long minute or more. But at last, voice now oddly gentle, "All right. Light down, son. We're going to sit here about an hour longer, let the horses have a good rest, then go on. Strip Latigo, give him a rubdown, and get some rest yourself."

Benteen had started pacing again. Mark noticed he was listening hard, hoping for the sound of a rider approaching through the darkness. But it did not come.

"Past dark, and he hasn't let her go," Benteen said, anxiety mixed with misery in his voice. "Lucas, I'm afraid—".

"So am I," Lucas said. "Afraid we made some mistake, so that he knows for sure we're after him, and won't let her go. Or else—"

He paused, obviously reluctant to finish what he had started to say. Benteen said tightly, "Or else what? Go ahead—tell me!"

"Or else," Lucas sighed, "he never had any intention of turning her loose so soon. We know now he's heading for that wild mesa country—so wild plenty have gotten lost in it. That might happen to Madge. When he does let her go, she might not be able to find her way out again. We have to think about that."

15   Trail Into Danger

That was a night which, it seemed to Mark, would never end.

It was very dark for a while. Then there was a moon, but only until a little past midnight. When it set, the stars were dimmed by high, drifting clouds, so that they did not offer much light. The dim boundaries of the horizons were all about, taking the form of a black, ragged line off to southward where the mesas began.

Those mesas were still some distance off. They were heading toward them on an angle toward the southeast, moving at a slow pace, Lucas in the lead, Benteen following him, Mark trailing behind his uncle.

Sometime after midnight, when they stopped again to rest, Benteen and Lucas had an argument about the direction they were taking.

"I say we should head straight for the mesas, get into them, then cut for their trail come first light," Benteen said. His anxiety was growing. His voice had become a harsh croak.

"I don't agree," Lucas told him. "It's my feeling that our one hope is to stay close enough so we can strike quick, from behind, when the night starts to break."

"But if he has changed direction on us!"

"Trav, I know those mesas. So does Cade, from all I've noticed so far. His trail showed him angling toward the wildest part of them, a country of deep crosshatched canyons. Even if he knows we're after him, I don't think Cade will change his plan—or his direction."

"Well, maybe so," Benteen muttered. "But there's also the chance he might have stopped for the night and we'll work on past him—"

"I don't think Cade will do any stopping—but that he'll push as hard as he can to get into the mesas, because once there the likelihood of him being overtaken becomes pretty faint, and he knows it. I'm counting on that to give us a chance. . . ."

Lucas paused for a long moment of listening hard, then went on, "I'm thinking about his horses. At the ranch, I noticed your black looked pretty worn. It seems that's likely, too, of his horse."

"Yes," Benteen admitted. "Cade and I have been doing a lot of hard riding on those two horses lately."

"He's going to have to stop somewhere and give them a good rest—is probably planning to put that off until he's in the mesas, but maybe they'll quit on him before then. I'm hoping so, anyway."

"Lucas, you've got to make me a promise," Benteen said. "When we do catch up, I get first crack at Cade!"

"Madge must be taken from him, safe and unharmed," Lucas said. "But I'm not promising you anything—about how we do that, or what comes later."

Mark had a feeling his father must be thinking of what he and Benteen had said to each other, back at the ranch before Cade's appearance. That situation hadn't changed any. Rescuing Madge was of first importance, of course, but afterward something still had to be done about Travis Benteen. As of the moment, a sort of truce existed between Lucas and the outlaw leader. When the truce ended, there was no telling what might happen. Both were strong, determined men.

They rode on, with the night blackness and silence

seeming to deepen, the country constantly growing rougher, one arroyo after another to scramble into and out of, gravelly flats between them—then even rockier going, with what seemed like stretches of slate cap where the footing was very uncertain.

Mark became very tired. His eyelids felt as though they had lead weights attached to them. Not only had it been many long hours since he had rolled out of his blankets yesterday, but the events of that day had drained him of emotion and energy.

He tried hard to stay awake and could not—dozed, and shook himself awake, only to doze again, swaying a little in the saddle, both hands gripping the horn.

Latigo paced steadily on. It was a time like this when care and kindness and the pains taken to train a good horse paid off. Latigo needed no constant urging to keep moving. He could be trusted not to stop.

When the little horse did halt, with Mark snapping fully awake, it was to discover Lucas had made another rest stop. His voice came in a low command: "Off saddle, son. We're going to take a breather of about half an hour this time."

Benteen muttered in protest, "Half an hour!"

"Trav, we've got to keep our horses as fresh as possible.

Get your rig off that pinto right now."

Mark stayed on his feet, kneading Latigo's leg and shoulder muscles. He knew that if he sat or lay down, he would be fast asleep once more within a minute.

Lucas and Benteen were conferring together again. The subject, this time, was the rifle, now in Sid Cade's possession.

" . . . Another rifle at the house, a Winchester, but with a broken ejector spring," Lucas remarked. "Of course, if I had known Mark would join us as he did, I'd have had him borrow a couple of rifles in town and bring them along. But I didn't know, and no use talking about it now."

"Never got in the habit of packing a saddle-gun," Benteen said, "and doubt if I'd be much good at using one, even if you had a Winchester to hand me right now."

"Trav, if we can't spot Cade and get close to him, in a hurry, he can hold us off with the rifle," Lucas said. "These two old Colt .45's we're packing haven't been used in years, and with their worn barrel grooves they're sure to throw wide beyond about forty yards."

Mark realized his father must be talking about two guns which had been mounted over the fireplace at the house for as long as he could remember. Lucas had packed them once, in the Nations and elsewhere, but put the Colts aside when he found greater accuracy and reliability in the rifle.

They were the only weapons with which Lucas and Benteen could have armed themselves, since, excepting the broken Winchester, there were no other guns at the ranch. And those two old Colts were liable to prove pretty uncertain if they had to be matched against Cade.

Benteen said, "Seems I heard somewhere you can fix up a stock for a handgun that'll give it the range of a rifle."

"No, Trav, you heard wrong," Lucas said. "I've seen such a stunt tried—had to attempt it myself once, as a matter of fact. A stock, even if you have one—and we don't—and can hold steady enough with it, will about double a handgun's effective range, which would still give you no more than fairly good accuracy at eighty to a hundred yards. And the rifle can find a man-sized target at up to half a mile."

"Which means we've got to sight Cade close enough so that these six-guns we're packing won't miss!" Benteen said. "Let's be moving on, and run him down!"

But Lucas made him wait the full half hour. By then the morning star was bright in the east and the air was very cool and sweet, with a faint thread of gray already showing against the eastern horizon. Mark resolved that now he was going to make it through until sunup with his eyes open.

But the lead weights tugged at them again; he nodded and sagged forward in saddle and slept—hard, this time.

There was a hazy realization, sometime later, that they had stopped and he was being lifted down. Mark tried to protest against this, to say he didn't need any babying, but he couldn't seem to get the words out.

The next thing he knew, Mark discovered himself stretched out on his side, a blanket spread over him, a saddle against his head as a pillow.

He threw the blanket aside and scrambled up. The time was now gray dawn, still not very light, but light enough for him to make out where he was: in a small natural cup that was bordered on three sides by rock masses fifty or so feet high. Off to one side, toward the south, the rising bluffs of the mesas were visible, now quite close, with deep weathered fissures or seams showing in them.

In the opposite direction, to the north, a trail led out of some thick brush. Mark figured they must have come along that trail. The three horses were in close to the towering rocks on the southern side of the cup, picketed and grazing.

There was no sign of his father and Travis Benteen.

Mark chewed a chunk of cold beef and a biscuit, washed down with a long swallow from his canteen. Only an occasional snort from one of the horses broke the deep dawn stillness.

It seemed obvious this had been picked as a good place to hide the horses, then work on afoot toward the mesas which began, Mark figured, not much more than a quarter of a mile away.

They did not soar up all at once from the plain, but rather in wave on wave of bluffs and ridges and sharp hogbacks—and for that matter the entire plain itself tilted up, along here, toward where those steep rises began.

Mark wondered whether something seen or heard had indicated the man they were after was yonder, close by. He waited awhile, with the light growing stronger. The eastern sky was turning rose and gold, and the sun would soon be up.

And nothing happened, nothing at all. Mark began to feel edgy. He walked around a bit, working the kinks out of his legs. At last he scrambled through and around the rocks at the southern side of the cup, found a way between them, and at last was almost in the open. There he paused to study the mesas.

Lucas had told him the word *mesa* meant "table" in Spanish, and from a distance they looked as flat at their highest points as so many table tops; but now Mark discovered they were uneven, with many irregular rises and dips.

The cattle trail used by the Texas herds wound through them somewhere off to the west. Along here they had the look of what Lucas had said they were: very wild country, great masses of soil and rock that were lifted from five to eight hundred feet above the plain.

All of the mesas together ran about a hundred miles from east to west and were about half of that width from north to south. There was a lot of room in them for somebody— Madge, for instance—to get lost.

Mark studied the nearest rise, which seemed to lift sheer for maybe a hundred feet or more. There appeared to be a ledge at its top, and beyond the ledge a ridge which was just this side of the first of the towering bluffs. At the bottom of the rise, where the plain ended, some trees showed, and there were more scattered between Mark and the rise itself, willows and cottonwoods and aspens and even some gnarled mesquites, although Lucas had remarked it was pretty far north hereabouts for mesquites to grow.

Something suddenly moved among the trees. Mark recognized Travis Benteen, bent almost double, leaving cover for a moment, hurrying toward a clump of brush, flattening himself out, pushing his way through. He reappeared, apparently working toward the base of that first rise.

Mark looked off to his right, then off to his left. It took several minutes of careful scrutiny before he discovered his father, because Lucas was moving with more care than Benteen, using every bit of cover to full advantage.

Lucas was at a distance of about a quarter of a mile east of Benteen, heading toward him. He appeared for a moment, straightening up, studying that rise ahead, then turned to Benteen with his arm lifted. It rose and fell twice, a signal that Benteen acknowledged at once with a return wave.

Then Lucas seemed to disappear. Mark knew he had not done that, but was only flattened out, even closer to the ground than Benteen, who was now on the move to join Lucas.

The sun was just up, a line of crimson against the eastern horizon. And Mark, looking up toward that first steep rise where the mesas began, caught his breath.

The dark figure of a man had suddenly appeared there,

silhouetted in the first light of the sun. He was standing on the ledge at the top of the rise. Mark could not make out who he was, but did not have to. Because his posture was a familiar one; he was holding a rifle with both hands, crosswise at waist level.

And Benteen was being careless, probably too much in a hurry or too worried after the careful search which had disclosed nothing. He was leaving the shelter of the trees and moving in the open, heading toward Lucas, calling something to him, maybe a demand that they get to the horses and push on into the mesas.

Sid Cade was standing about a hundred feet above him, probably three or four times that far away, Lucas' rifle in his hands.

Mark left the shelter of the rocks and started running forward. He shouted, "Uncle Trav! Look out—above you!"

Benteen wheeled toward him, and Mark pointed up toward that ledge. Benteen's head snapped around. He discovered the man.

Cade pulled the rifle's trigger, with its familiar whiplashing sound, its echoes that went rippling away. Mark saw Benteen spin around and go headfirst into what seemed to be either a hollow or an arroyo yonder.

Lucas opened up with his six-gun, firing fast. Mark saw dust spurt on the slope below Cade. A slide showed there, loose earth where part of the ledge above had crumbled and fallen down. Those bullet spurts seemed to march up that slide part way toward Cade, but not quite to the top. Cade fired again, the rifle swinging. He was aiming now at Lucas.

Mark was still running forward, zigzagging. He could see Cade more clearly, with the fast-growing light from the sun—and also had a sudden glimpse of Madge, beyond the man, moving there for a moment before she vanished from sight. Cade fired again at Lucas.

Benteen shouted, "Here, boy!" He was hugging the far bank of a dry arroyo that was barely deep enough to give him shelter, and he had turned his head for a second, with an urgent, beckoning wave of his arm. Mark went into the arroyo, landed in its sandy bed, rolled and scrambled up to his feet, and plunged on to hug the bank beside Benteen, who lifted his gun, fired twice, then cried out angrily.

"I'm not coming anywhere near him!"

Mark ventured a hurried, cautious look over the rim of the bank. His angle of vision up to that ledge was now so

narrow that he did not see Cade at all, but the wasping crack of the rifle again warned him the man was still there. Mark did not hear the bullet. Lucas still seemed to be Cade's target.

Then it fell quiet. Benteen sighted with his gun, but shook his head. He looked toward the left. After a moment Mark saw his father coming toward the two of them, working quickly but carefully along the arroyo, crouching down but keeping sharp watch on the ledge above.

"You all right, Trav?" he called, approaching.

"Yes," Benteen answered. "Thanks to Mark. If he hadn't yelled when he did, I'd have been knocked over like a sitting duck."

Lucas did not comment that Benteen would not have been in such danger if he had taken more care. Instead, Mark's father put a hand on his son's shoulder for a second.

In that hand Mark felt a slight quiver. Lucas was not afraid for himself. It was Mark's presence here, necessary though this was to save Benteen from his own recklessness, which bothered him.

And a glance back by Lucas to where he had left Mark, with a shake of his head, showed that he was considering and discarding the possibility of Mark returning there, that

Cade couldn't be trusted to let him return untouched.

"This is just the way you were afraid it might be when we caught up with him, Lucas—that he might move a little too fast for us, get to that higher country first and hold the upper hand," Benteen remarked unsteadily. "It's just the way you said."

Lucas nodded grimly. "He has all the advantage—not only the rifle but that downhill angle as well."

Lucas had once commented to Mark that in a fight a man who could get above his opponent always held a big edge. Trying to cope with him was like throwing rocks up from the bottom of a well.

"Also, there are some boulders scattered along that ledge," Lucas continued. "He has plenty of cover."

Mark ventured another look. He had a glimpse of several of those boulders. And he drew a bullet from the rifle, which made him duck fast.

Lucas put his hand on Mark's shoulder again. "Stay down, son."

"What do you make the distance to that ledge?" Benteen asked.

"Straight line from here? Over a hundred yards, maybe as much as a hundred and fifty," Lucas answered.

It meant they couldn't bring their guns to bear on it with any hope of accuracy.

Benteen said then, "Madge! If I only knew she was there!"

"She is," Mark told him. "I saw her."

Benteen started to lift himself, a furious move as though he meant to leave the arroyo. Lucas grabbed at him. "Stay put, Trav! Getting yourself shot isn't going to help her any!"

As though to emphasize that statement, two bullets from the rifle ripped dirt from the rim of the arroyo bank, just above their heads.

Benteen chewed his lip. He had a wild, frantic look. The thought of his daughter, so near and yet so far beyond his reach, was ripping at him cruelly. "Lucas, you and I could spread out, rush him, up that slide. One of us might make it!"

"No," Lucas said. "He'd get us both before we even reached the bottom of the slide."

"But what are we going to do?" Benteen cried.

"I don't know," Lucas said.

"We can't stay here!"

But the rifle cracked again, ripping more dirt from the

arroyo rim, and Travis Benteen knew there was nothing else they could do. As things stood, Cade, with the rifle, could hold them off as long as he wished. They couldn't get any closer to him than they were now.

16   A Deadly Game

Cade suddenly shouted, voice contemptuous, jeering, "So you wouldn't listen to what I said, not to follow me! Well, sit there and stew. When I'm ready to leave, I will— and the girl goes with me. I'll turn her loose, somewhere in the canyons. Then try to find her!"

Benteen leaned against the bank, head on his arm. His shoulders shook at that threat.

Lucas was looking about. Mark knew he was thinking, hard and fast, seeking some way to end this deadlock.

Cade sent two more shots at them.

Benteen turned his lined, haggard face toward Lucas. "He's using a lot of shells. Your rifle must be almost empty. And when it is!"

"Trav, I wouldn't count on that," Lucas said. "Cade has shown he's a man who plans ahead. He made up his mind

to own the rifle. That kind of man would have supplied
himself with extra shells for it."

Then Lucas moved a little closer to Benteen. "I've been
thinking about the reason he's staying there and shooting
at us, instead of pulling out. It must be what I figured last
night—his horses need rest. He has to wait on them, until
they're fit for more hard going—"

"So what?" Benteen muttered. "We still can't get at
him."

"Not from here," Lucas admitted. "But—how did he
make it up to that ledge? I scouted at least two miles east
and didn't spot any trail leading to it. More, the ledge
plays out in that direction. So he must have ridden in from
the west."

Benteen was listening with new hope. "Go on, Lucas!"

"I'll work off along the arroyo, try to find that trail,
follow it, and get close to him on the ledge. You stay here
and burn powder, keep him shooting at you. Move around
a little, make him think it's both of us sniping at him."

"No!" Benteen said. "You stay and let me go!"

Lucas shook his head. "You're too worked up against
him, Trav, too liable to make some wild move that will
betray you."

He paused, lips tightly compressed for a moment, then continued, "Besides, it's my job to handle. I ordered those rest stops last night, to keep ourselves and our horses fresh for whatever might come at dawn. If we hadn't done any stopping, it might have meant Cade could have been cut off before he reached the trail up to the ledge. The move was a mistake. I made it—"

"Lucas, don't rawhide yourself," Benteen said.

"I'm not. We're being handed another chance: Cade's need to wait until his horses are rested. But if we wait, too, let him hold us here until he rides on, I don't think we'll be able to catch up with him again. He has to be stopped right now, before another day, and I'm the one who must do it."

Lucas glanced toward Mark, then, started to say something more, but shook his head and left them, bent almost double, hurrying away along the arroyo's shallow course to the west. Benteen began immediately to work his six-gun, firing up at the ledge, hugging the bank as quick answering bullets came back from Cade.

Benteen shifted position, farther along the bank, and fired again. He paused to shake spent shells from his gun and to reload. Cade raked the bank. It must be as Lucas had said, Mark thought—he had plenty of bullets for the rifle.

Mark looked after his father, with a realization of how dangerous the part was that Lucas had assigned himself to play in this deadly game.

It was one thing to speak of finding a trail and working up it, onto the ledge, for a try at Cade. It would be another thing to make such a try work against the rifle, armed with an old six-gun whose worn barrel grooves would make it throw wide.

Mark backed off, a step away from Travis Benteen, then another step. He began to put distance between himself and the man, working eastward along the arroyo.

Benteen, busy with his task of keeping all of Cade's attention concentrated on himself, did not notice what Mark was doing. Mark turned and began to move faster, straight toward the sun, which was now fully up, sending its crimson heat directly into his eyes.

There was no sure idea in him of what he was going to do, or how—only the thought hammering hard of the danger Lucas was going to face when he tried to drive at Cade on the ledge.

Maybe, Mark told himself, he could get up there, in

a way denied to Lucas and Benteen because of their size, just to be there when his father made his try, to offer some help—maybe a yell at the crucial moment to distract Cade's attention, turn the man from Lucas toward him, give Lucas the opportunity for what he had to do . . . .

Mark knew well enough it was a wild plan, with only about one chance in a hundred of succeeding. He knew what Lucas would say if he were aware of what his son had in mind.

Still, Mark had to try it. He couldn't wait with Benteen and do nothing. He just couldn't. The odds were too great against Lucas succeeding in his perilous attempt if there wasn't help of some kind for him, up on the ledge.

The arroyo swung in a wide bend toward the rising ridge. Mark worked along the inner bank. He had put about fifty yards between himself and Benteen, who was firing fast again, using up bullets.

Mark found himself suddenly wondering how many of those bullets were left for Benteen to use. The outlaw was wearing a shell belt. Its loops had been fairly full when all this started—.45 calibre shells, which fitted the two six-guns—but there was a limit to how long those shells would last, and Benteen must be coming close to it.

The arroyo began to bend back, and Mark realized he was as close to the ridge as he was going to get. He stopped and studied its steeply lifting face. After several moments of looking, he found what he had hoped would be there.

It was a fissure, a gully, gouged out by the runoffs of many rains—deep enough to hide him, Mark hoped. Looking up, he saw it ran all the way to the ledge. About a hundred-foot climb . . . .

And nothing was to be gained by any further study. There was an open space between the arroyo and the base of the ridge which had to be crossed. Mark drew a deep breath, scrambled out of the arroyo, and began to run as he had never run before.

It hadn't looked far, that distance between the arroyo and the base of the ridge, but it seemed to stretch out before him as he ran. Mark felt as though one of Nils Swenson's anvils was attached to each of his feet, as though he was making more noise than a team of pounding freighter horses.

And no use zigzagging, because Cade was off to his right, not in front of him; zigzagging wouldn't help in the least. He had to run straight—and he covered the last ten feet or so in a flattened-out dive that landed him on his stomach where the gully began.

Mark hugged the ground, then, gasping for air, sucking it in through his mouth. The temptation was great just to stay there for a while until he was breathing normally again, until he was completely sure Cade hadn't noticed what he was doing.

But Lucas, he told himself, wasn't wasting any time in what he was attempting, and there was no sense at all in Mark's trying to do this unless he made it up to the ledge before Lucas came along from the other direction. Mark began to climb.

It was rough going, because of the ridge's steep rising angle. He had to claw his way up, pull himself along with knees and elbows, boot toes digging in—he slid back a little twice in the first twenty feet, dirt and pebbles trickling down, making a racket that seemed to Mark as loud as a waterfall.

He managed to stop himself, both times, to recover and keep going, because he must. The eroded gully was deep enough, barely so, to hide him. Neither Lucas nor Benteen could have used it. They would have been exposed.

The angle of climb seemed to grow even steeper. He came to a clump of dry, thorny brush, growing in the gully itself,

and had to force his way through. Dust tickled his nostrils. He sneezed, hard, then held his breath, rigid for a moment, sure Cade must have heard him. But Cade apparently hadn't, and Mark moved on.

Somewhere during the course of that furious climb, Benteen suddenly shouted, anxiety and fright in his voice, calling to Mark. He shouted again, several times. Mark kept going.

And all at once, when it seemed he had been at it for hours, he discovered that he had reached the ledge.

Mark stayed in the gully for a moment longer, while he ventured a cautious look.

Cade was visible, off to his right, down on one knee in the shelter of some boulders. Mark saw him thrust the rifle barrel forward and fire. Cade shouted tauntingly. Two six-gun blasts answered him.

More of those boulders, singly and in clumps, were scattered along the ledge, as Lucas had remarked. There was one nearby. Mark scrambled up from the gully, onto the ledge, and ran for it.

Moving on tiptoe, he made as little noise as possible— but again it seemed to him the pounding of his boots must be audible for at least a mile. He threw himself at the boulder and hugged it, the rock already hot from the sun. But Mark didn't mind that.

Another cautious look; Cade was still on one knee, with no indication he had heard anything.

Mark looked farther along the ledge, which seemed to run for a considerable distance to the west. Lucas was not in sight, anywhere.

He picked another boulder, sprinted to it, hugged rock again, much closer to Cade now. Perspiration was streaming down Mark's face, though he felt cold, not hot. He wiped his face with both hands, and for the first time discovered he had lost his hat, somewhere since leaving Travis Benteen.

And he couldn't stay here; he had to be much closer to Sid Cade when Lucas came along. Mark moved again, this time diving in among several boulders that were somewhat back on the ledge.

It was even hotter among these boulders, so hot the air he sucked into his lungs made them burn. But he forgot this discomfort, his heart lurching violently, as Cade spoke with sudden harshness: "What's that?"

Mark was close to the man now, for he heard the question clearly—and also heard Madge answer him: "It—

it's just the horses, Mr. Cade."

No further sound for a long moment, while Mark held his breath. Then Cade grunted, apparently accepting her explanation. The rifle barked. Cade yelled, "Come on, Benteen, stick your head up—you're wasting my time—give me a clear aim at you!"

Benteen's gun crashed. Cade laughed mockingly. "Nowhere near me! And you never will be!"

Mark worked his way around one of the boulders. All at once he discovered that he was looking right at Madge, and she was looking back at him.

The girl was a little off to his left—must have been aware of his approach for several moments, Mark realized, and had covered for him when Cade had heard the scraping sound of his boots.

Madge sent a frightened look toward Cade, then glanced over to Mark again, lifting a finger hurriedly to her lips.

Mark had to clamp his teeth hard together to keep from uttering a wild laugh. If there was one warning he didn't need, it was one to keep as quiet as possible.

Madge was about a dozen yards from him, standing. Beyond her were the two horses, their heads down—worn, as Lucas had predicted they would be, needing the rest they were getting now. Cade could do no more traveling until they were in better shape.

The girl looked tired, also, with dark hair wispy about her dirt-smudged cheeks. Her skirt and jacket and blouse were soiled. But something in the firmness of Madge's chin, the tilt of her head, told Mark she had lost none of her spunk.

Beyond the horses there was the further lift of the ridge to the nearby mesas, with a sort of saddle-shaped notch scooped out of it, an old faint trail leading up over that hollow. Cade was probably planning to go in that direction, on into the mesas, when he left this stopping place, Mark thought.

There was still no sign of Lucas anywhere, no sound to break the quiet until Benteen pulled trigger again.

Cade fired in response. Then the man stirred, backing up, remaining hunched down until he was clear of the rim of the ledge. He straightened up, sorted bullets from a jacket pocket, and reloaded the rifle. Meanwhile, he was keenly studying the ledge, where it ran off to westward.

When he turned to take a look toward the east, Mark sighed with relief, crouching in the nest of boulders.

He heard the crunch of Cade's boots, heard the man

laugh. "Thought for a while McCain might be having the fool notion he could follow me up the trail, get close enough from the west to make his six-gun effective. Sure wish he had tried it!"

Mark started. Then Cade spoke again.

"He must have had a rush of good sense to his head, though," the man said. "I just had a glimpse of him, down there with your pa—"

For a second, everything seemed to tilt and slide away from Mark. He felt cold, and sick, and terribly afraid.

All of the effort he had made had been in vain. Lucas was not on the ledge, but down in the arroyo. For some reason, he had turned back. Mark was here, alone, within reach of this cruel man who held the rifle.

And a moment later it grew even worse. For the crunch of Cade's boots began once more, and he was coming straight toward the cluster of boulders where Mark was hiding!

They were only about waist-high to Cade. A couple of steps closer and he would be looking right down at Mark, who closed his eyes and waited.

Cade stopped. A chink of metal sounded. He spoke again, "The two of them down there, like coyotes driven

into their den, afraid to come out—your famous pa and
Lucas McCain! Oh, and that McCain punk kid too!"

Mark's fists clenched angrily. He opened his eyes and
started to rise. If he was to be discovered, he might as well
try to get in a couple of licks, as a response to that slurring
remark, not be dragged out . . . .

Cade was moving away from him, toward the horses—
past Madge, who stepped aside. The man lifted a canteen
from the saddle horn of his horse, unscrewed it and tilted
the canteen, his head back, drinking.

The rifle was no more than half a dozen feet from Mark.
Cade had left it there, leaning against one of the boulders.

He still had two handguns on him, his own and the one
taken from Travis Benteen.

Madge sent an urgent look at Mark, a look at the rifle.
He nodded, gestured to her as he started to move, a gesture
warning Madge to get well out of the way.

Instead, she turned and ran at Cade, leaping at him
from behind, wrapping both arms about his arms. She
screamed, "Run, Mark!"

Cade reacted instantly, in wild fury, flailing his arms
to throw her off. Mark ran at the rifle. He grabbed it up,
veered and raced across the ledge.

Those boulders which had shielded Cade were now in his way. He started to scramble up over them.

Madge cried out again. And Cade shouted. Then one of his six-guns blasted, driving a bullet at Mark McCain.

17   Right, All the Way!

Mark heard the bullet strike against rock and scream off, ricocheting away. He leaped out into space—he was falling! He hit hard on the dirt slide and pitched on down, rolling over and over, helpless to stop himself, the rifle cradled against his body, battering him at every turn.

A long fall, before he slid to a stop and scrambled up shakily. Cade's handgun was thunderous above him, with dust spurting all about on the slide.

Lucas cried, "Mark!" He turned and saw his father coming, long legs scissoring fast, hands reaching out. Mark lifted the rifle. He threw it to his father, who made a quick catch, hands in a lightning shift, swinging it into firing position, aiming upward.

Then he was using it as only Lucas McCain could, working the ejector lever, with bullets pouring from its muzzle,

273

streaking up at the ledge where Cade in his shouting rage stood fully exposed, Lucas' keen eyes guiding them in their unerring mission.

Mark saw Sid Cade shudder and bend, saw him take a faltering step forward, saw the man pull trigger a last time, one final bullet which went nowhere. Then he toppled off the ledge also, the same hard fall Mark had just experienced, coming on down in explosive clouds of dust, rolling over and over.

Until, at last, a sliding stop, only a dozen feet away, with Lucas holding the rifle alertly ready if it should be needed again.

But Sid Cade did not get up, as Mark had. He would never get up. His evil had ended here.

Mark turned away, shivering. Lucas moved quickly to him. "Son, you've taken quite a beating. Here, lean on me."

"No, sir." He could hardly speak, his throat was raw and dust-choked, but he managed to keep his voice firm. "Madge is up there. I've got to go and help her down."

And he did, though things seemed rather blurred for a while. There was only one thing more that Mark remembered of the events at that place.

It happened a little later, all of them standing together.

Travis Benteen's arm was about his daughter's shoulders. She looked toward the slide, then shuddered and put her face against his shirt.

Lucas spoke, voice quiet but stern, "Trav, you're looking at what is going to be your own end if you don't give yourself up, right now. And do you want Madge's and Susan's last memory of you to be like that?"

Travis Benteen's face was drawn and bleak. When his answer came it was very low, but they all heard it. "No, Lucas," he said. "You're right, all the way. I'll ride back with you."

The two McCains headed home together at dusk that evening.

A long day behind them, and a lot more that had happened. Mark was sorting those events out now in his memory as he and his father paced along quietly together.

There had been the return to the ranch, which took up much of the day. When they reached home, it was to find a surprise waiting—people moving about, keeping watch on things.

Nils Swenson had explained it simply, "You told us not to send help when you were here watching, yourself, Lucas.

But with you gone it was a different matter. We came out to make sure nobody with wrong ideas tried to take advantage of that."

They headed on to town, then, and there was the reunion of Madge and her mother, of Benteen and his wife, and of Susan Benteen saying, smiling though her eyes were damp, "I'm so glad, Lucas. It's the end of a nightmare. Now we'll be together again—Trav, Madge, and myself—in peace, some day . . . ."

Micah had come along with news of his own. He and his posse had taken the other three men of the Benteen bunch. Most of their loot had been recovered. "Trav," he had said, "I guess we had better go along. No need to worry about your trying to get away?"

"Micah, nothing on earth could make me try to run now!" Benteen had said, smiling. "Let's go."

They had left together, curious onlookers stepping aside to let them pass. The town was very quiet. There was talk that Pete Nader had left North Fork, heading for elsewhere.

Then Dr. Harvey had claimed Mark, to do some patching on his bruises and cuts, with Mrs. Harvey also fussing over him. After that he had a few minutes with Madge,

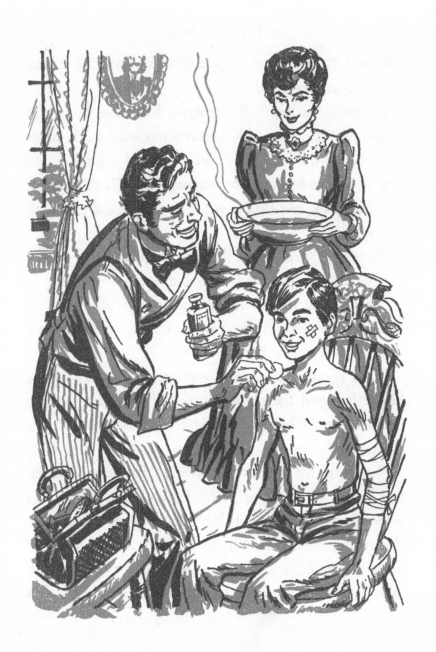

who said, "Mark, coming up to that ledge was the bravest thing anybody ever did!"

He shook his head. Even braver had been her act in rushing at Sid Cade. Mark was certain now he would never have made it but for Madge's help. He tried to put this into words. Madge blushed, interrupting him, "Let's not talk about it. Look, can I come out to the ranch and ride with you again?"

"Sure!" he said. "And I'll leave Latigo in town for you."

"Oh, no!" she protested. "Not your Latigo!"

But he insisted, and Madge finally agreed. He could make do with the pinto for a while. Latigo, with his gentle habits, was the right horse for her.

Lucas rejoined him, then, and they started for home. His father eyed the pinto thoughtfully, glanced back to Latigo left at the Madera House hitch-rail, but had no comment to make.

Not about that, at least; he revealed that Susan Benteen and Madge would stay in North Fork until it was decided where Benteen's trial would take place, which would probably require about a month; then they would go to where he had to serve his sentence and settle down nearby, with Mrs. Benteen taking a job to support them, until his debt was discharged and he was free again.

It meant Madge would be visiting the ranch often, Mark thought, and found he was looking forward to that. They would do a lot of riding together.

Lucas fell silent, then.

He had already explained why he had not appeared on the ledge—that he had not been able to spot the trail leading to it, then had heard Benteen shouting Mark's name and had turned back, with cold fear for his son. He had rejoined Benteen only moments before Cade placed the rifle where Mark could seize it.

The rifle was across Lucas' saddle horn now, where it belonged. And there was one more thing to be said. Mark had been waiting all day for Lucas to say it. At last, when their place came in sight, he did.

"About your going up on that ledge, son—" His manner indicated he had given this a lot of thought.

And he went on, "I know why you did it, Mark—to help me. I'm pretty proud you ran such a risk for that reason. But—must I point out you should have stayed put, no matter what you were thinking, because I would have wanted it exactly that way?"

"I knew I was going against what you would want, Pa,

but I had to do it," Mark replied. "And I guess I would have to do the same thing if it happened again—"

He caught himself, with the reminder that he was saying too much.

Except that he had to make one thing clear. "I'm not trying to get off being punished, if you think that's needful. You've always said a man must do what he feels is right, then stand by it. I'm standing by what I did."

Lucas was chewing his lip. He sighed, showing a rueful smile. "It's coming to me that if anybody is to blame, I am —because of teaching you that! I can't say I'm sorry you've learned so well. . . . Punishment? No. Unless one thing should happen—"

"I think I know what you mean," Mark said. "If I should ever brag about getting the rifle back. But I won't."

"Good. Now, let's forget it," Lucas said. "What happened today was ugly, but had to be. There are ugly things in this life—many more, though, that are good. Look for the good ones. Forget all that's ugly, as fast as you can."

He glanced ahead. They were on their own broad acres, which had been wasteland when Lucas first arrived here, bringing a very young Mark McCain with him.

They had come a long way, since. They would go a

lot farther. Lucas was thinking about that. "Come fall, after we make our beef sales and are set for the winter," he said, "I think it will be time to file for another quarter-section, then start working it next spring."

He smiled at his son. "You're getting so you can handle more every day, Mark. There's got to be plenty of room for all that both of us will want to do!"

Yes, they would go far, would grow, as did the ranch, because it was in them to work and build. It wouldn't be easy. Nothing that was worthwhile ever came easy. But no matter what came, their feet would always be firmly planted on their own land.

They would make out. The rifle, resting across Lucas' saddle horn, guaranteed that.

Then, studying the rifle, Mark realized it was nothing by itself. What gave it power were the strong hands which held it, the keen eyes which sighted it, the canny, sharp but compassionate mind which planned its use.

All those belonged to Lucas McCain. And Mark said, "Pa, do you think I can ever be as good a man as you?"

"Why, son," his father answered, "if you don't grow up to be a much better man than I am, I'm going to be awfully disappointed!"

It sounded like a lot to expect of him, Mark thought. But he would do his best. His very best.

They rode into the yard and dismounted, then, with the great pleasure of being home.

Made in the USA
Las Vegas, NV
17 January 2024

84362047R00166